UNBATHED BRAINS

POEMS

FROM MINNESOTA AND THE MILKY WAY

Hari Hyde

Library of Congress Control Number: 2023910653

ISBN: 979-8-9867181-4-9

Published in Middletown, DE

Book Cover Design by ebooklaunch.com

CONTENTS

MINNESOTA

Ten thousand years later, the craters
of gadabout glaciers cradled
ten thousand lakes.

Bunyanesque ice plowed and scraped
pits, hollows, and furrows, lugging
and leaving gravel and boulders for sport.

Envisage grand graves filled with frolic,
when glacial gravediggers' spades melted,
drenching the trenches with waterworks,

sloshing liquid elixirs in crannies and clefts,
dousing the depths of the dents,
raising rainy revivals to rinse sunken saucers,

flooding the fathoms of gargantuan gashes,
dunking the deep dimples in prodigious puddles,
sprinkling soused sprites in each burrow and breach,

streaming blue waves over iced behemoths' graves,
showering bustling buckets of pure, plunging potions,
flowing fleet fluid over each nick in the notches,

ladling lakes in the lush land
of ten thousand wet worlds,
royal realms with rippling lids.

Fling fish into the fresh froth
near the phantasmagoria of forests,
with fierce beasts that deplore us.

Travel the world, you'll not feel it—
the lake archangels that elate us.
On a brisk autumn eve,

lakes exhale a hypnotic haze,
an aura to hearten the heavens,
an inexplicable esprit in the air.

Only mercurial Minnesota can seize it,
then awaken a winter to freeze it.
Wondrous wild wafts from the lakes.

No holes inhabit this heartland,
nothing but dippers
and big boisterous baths.

THE MILKY WAY

A night sky glitters and glides,
steadfast, sincere, and shy.
Long light years sanction surety.
Stars settle, approachably nearby.

Then out from heaven's harvest,
snowflakes festoon the plains in privacy.
Beneath the muddled moon, all masonry
crouches—contorted and costumed.

Snow imps pinch my skin's veneer.
Snowdrifts grunt beneath my boots.
How unlike the stars in distant geniality,
alights the snooping snow in intimacy!

Spangles in a snowbank glisten,
imploring I look, insisting I listen,
not flickering as do far-flung suns,
whose habitation harbors in my passions.

Yet how oft have neighbors gazed at me,
afar, and distinguished my ghost so lucidly,
ne'er lighting upon the lather in its luster!
We deepen each depth the closer we've crept.

THE SCRIPT

Memory mounts as a scurrilous script
and clings as a shadow shed solely for one,
a ghostwriter gathering the pages you ripped
from dirt that you've done and lies that you've spun.

Bygone releases the beast
prowling the precinct of singular souls,
foraging forgone, forlorn fancies, to feast
upon truth in the troughs, goals in the bowls.

Chained to the savage,
leashed to the prophetic past,
we're racked and wrecked by its ravage.
Denounce the director. Deliver the cast.

CIRCUS BALLOON

At eleven, I was bused to the circus
with boys and girls of my kind.
I don't remember the tigers,
or clowns or trapeze or elephants.

I remember the end of the circus,
waiting outside for the bus,
watching someone release a buoyant balloon.
It bothered me to see the balloon wasted,

and I wondered if he would go to the wrong places.
I felt scared for the balloon because he was helpless.
He soared up with confidence, though,
but then just lounged around in the low sky.

I felt unsettled, for I forecast a finale, a quick end,
either a launch through the clouds,
or a bursting in air.
After a while, I adapted to dashed expectations.

This balloon was well balanced.
This balloon adjusted to his modern milieu.
Who first fancied to force helium gas
into a plastic wrapper?

But then to think this big bubble
would hover at the hem of the heavens!
Would dally in a perfect dance under the clouds!
Everything turns out just right for someone else.

GRAND CANYON VACANCY

A void with a vacancy,
A hint at infinity,
A space fillable
With fancy.

My leap from the ledge
Could cork its concavity.
I'd finally find a space
Fit for sublimity.

At the sun's radiant rising,
In the rib of the furrow,
Fire flares in the fissure,
A flame in the pit.

When Nature is Grand,
She hands some to Man,
To me and the meager,
A gulp in Her gullet.

Reverence rings, raining
Upon the rent in the rock,
To fill in the fracture
And bloom up the burrow.

I'd take the north rim to gab
Upon the girth of the cathedral,
And the south rim
To swallow the hollow.

No one knows the cause of the canyon.
Don't trust the government guiders
Or the local insiders. Don't listen
To one thing but its gurgling spring.

It ain't a real river from up here.
It ain't got an anger.
It ain't divulging the depth
Of the ditch and the den.

Canyon crickets choired in a shower of stones.
They contemplate time, more than most.
I'm saying they're crickets,
And not quanta of space bits.

Snaps in my campfire snuck
From gaps in the wood.
Wherever light brightens the black,
It all starts with a crack.

Luster launches down
Trenches and troughs,

Down frays in the drapery,
Down the carved cave of creation,

Down curtains of canyon,
Chronicling stratified streamers,
Still sliding, digging, eroding,
Past a canyon coyote.

Don't trust this mule.
I don't like his eyes.
I'm walking him down
And watching, besides.

I'm watching and listening
To the sonorous somewhere,
To somewhere swelling near here,
To the roaring, arousing this resonant dent.

The west sun chases its shadows
Across quilts of the desert,
Across the vent of this void.
Shadows churn in this chamber,

Tumbling a tunneling wind in the chasm,
Flapping my jacket in a galloping spasm.
I squint through an abyss
And glimpse the Proprietor.

GOURMAND UNDER THE GRILL

The best bites
were relished by the gourmand
under the tangerine tresses.

Ah! 'twould do me to fondle and feast
on that same bloody cow muscle
this fiery phantom's now a-nibblin'.

The flames inflict a quick lick without chewing,
but snitch the vital vim of the vittles.
That ghost can sure savor a steak!

Jump up from yer cage! Do the bars of that grill
frame the flicked fire as my prisoner,
or is it me on the flip side who's serving the time?

Release the steak to my plate,
caked with yer charred, cheap saliva
where the pretty pink frosting should be.

Be ya built of hot rocks, or gas in the draft,
or just insane in yer wild mustard mane
and blazin' red bristles for whiskers,

that portion ye've canceled
goes wantin' still on my tongue,
slinging my remembers in embers.

Ya keep spewing yer spatter
to eat the elite of my meat.
This orange glutton can't gain

an ounce on her paunch.
Ten steaks on the grill
and she's still slipping her corset.

My steak is half et,
but I won't give that troll
'neath the grate a damp word.

I can sanction the sin that occurred.
When you feed second to fire,
remember those who feed third.

ERSTWHILE ALL THE WHILE

If Death's cart rolls along time,
I will wait to continue.
I am not late to contribute
if I am dead a long time.
At last, lasting last, to luxuriate,
irrefutably dead,

certainly dead, and continually dead.
Eternity certifies the improbable life,
untroubled by dying,
advancing still in perpetually dead.
Once I lodged laughingly alive.
And preceding this?

I dwelt as deniable as they.
Empty though never abandoned,
available but inaccessible,
indivisible and indisposed.
I mock the not-ever invented.
These never-things rue

that I'd unlatched the hatch
while they press against the door,
wait to be born,
await formulation.

Kick yourself nowhere. I cannot help.
As eternal royalty in our rivalry,

I win every contention
over the pretenders from elsewhere.
I now spread sharp elbows,
sealing the cracks to your coming,
though you're chipping new nicks in my bones
where you never stopped drumming.

Modest in life. Now I am gloating.
I am affirmed dead a long time.

REPORT CARD

On my high school report card,
I would almost always get A's.
I felt no pride in this,
as I strived for success in the real world.

After three decades in this real world,
I learned, in all candor,
we will always be failures,
no matter what we achieve.

Goals are elastic and gusty
in the real-world arcade.
And failed projects bring joy
for the hope of a new project.

For that reason, I look back
upon my life's great satisfaction
in earning those A's
in high school.

I wear my copper Honor Student pin
on my white baseball cap.
The copper got green. Its gravitas grew grand.
I'd kept this pin in a drawer for thirty years.

Now I enjoy its pristine plateau
that cannot be exceeded.
No one gets hoisted higher
than the ceiling.

My hope is that Heaven
harbors no grade
more majestic than "A"
written down.

HOW TO LIE

Come in, ye lads,
who take swigs of sweethearts and swag.
I'll tell ye once ye needs to double yer bads.
Ye din e'en know how to brag.

A boast don't grow landlubber tame.
A brag slides its feet
and oozes and ahhhs yer name
and can't keep yer crowin' discreet.

Ye seadogs 'r' floatin'
wit' yer meat hooks fer matey.
But fer landlubber-like boatin',
the bustle of beddin' gets weighty.

In the foam of the briny,
yer keepin' yer diddlin' dry.
Ye don't know yer hook from yer heinie,
and ye din e'en yet learn how to lie.

Ain't no bloke who what mires
his least leg in the one mute maw of a lass
who can slow the stride of his desires
for more muck, more moor, morass.

Hope that yer hearin' the guts of my gloat,
what falls wet as a whisper and soft as a bayou,
as we ain't confessin' it was sung in my throat,
for I'm learnin' ye how to commence lettin' a lie go.

A lyin' bog preys on rain for its slush.
A lyin' fen licks likker from a vale and a swale.
A lyin' marsh lies green in a brackish brown brush.
A lyin' swamp moors mangroves in its lyin' pail.

Then that's it, all ye lads and near thinkers.
Remember to slather some sly mud in yer airs.
The deeper the slough, the softer the sinkers.
And a limey's alit by the sand what he wears.

MERCIFUL & MIGHTY

In a childhood relay race,
the last leg matched me
with a slow friend,
who I then let win,
by slowing my gait.

It meant something to him to win,
but nothing to me to lose,
this time.

I plod the pendulous pathway of charity.
I am an heir and apostle of rescue.
I am a beneficiary and profiteer
of clemency.

Above all,
I seek mercy
of He who is Mighty.

I wonder if my mercy
streams in the wind,
to be captured and clutched
in the palm of His hand.

I forebode the coming applause,
as I await His hands clapping.

SCIENCE FAIR

A mouse in our closet
used my imagination.
I saw us as partners
in my science fair project.

I jailed him, alive,
the fool for the food.
I thought about him
with each wedge of my woodworking,
building each berth in his box.

I created this maze as a lab,
not a labyrinth.
A pattern of pattering alleys,
a passage of chambers,
a panic of halls,
a quandary of cubicles,
a muddled, meandering, and quizzical quest.

Find the cheese.
A riddle to delight
the winding wanderings
of my assistant,
the mouse.

On opening night,
my mouse escaped
as he was lowered
into the maze.

And I presented only
an empty segmented box
at the science fair,
ready to explain how
it was intended to work.

I spied storms through the school windows.
Those slices of lightning
showed me our reflection
on the radiant panes.

Showed me the boy with the box
and looming life's fleeting audience.
Our Creator menaced my barren arena,
casting His canopy of imposed inspiration.

UNBATHED BRAINS

Unbathed, my brain basin hankered for brew,
poured pints, drizzled drafts, to drown it anew,
as I swam without a lifeguard in a lager-laced pool
and balanced my butt on my favorite barstool.

Parley with barley. Exalt with a malt.
Feast with the yeast. The beast is at fault
for fomenting a fellow's frisky freefall
and convivial crawl to cuddly, bubbly alcohol.

My pint of stout left five foamy rings,
to measure the motion of my flappable wings
that sprouted spontaneously in Doghead Bar,
where homebrew recasts my near as afar.

After my second pint, I reported the weather,
in Gaithersburg, in my brain's lustrous leather:
cloudy with a boozy breeze fluffing a feather,
but sunny, too, calm and clement, altogether.

Then raindrops tinkled through the patio shade,
as though clouds renounced each petite renegade.
On tables, on chairs, a barrage bounced up and blinked,
and jolly jets of brief bubbles rebounded and winked

at me, who beheld their pitch and their plummet.
I discerned the drops dive and vacate their summit,
to refute my wisdom's unwise weather forecast,
to alert me to regard my life's rumpus roar past,

to instruct me on the straight and the narrow,
to warn me, my third draft might hasten to harrow
my reverent route, the avenue of angelic arrows,
straighter than streaks and springs of the sparrows.

The raindrops arranged like pale prison bars,
a fence commencing from strewn, streaming stars,
as though these liquid lines conspired to jail me,
as though elixir beer could flounder and fail me.

I'm bathed in my brain and soaked in my throat.
I've bombarded my belly with beer, near to float.
I envisioned I'm thin. I fantasized that I'm fast.
I fancied to slip through life's jail bars at last.

So, outside, homeward I ran: ready, set, and get wet.
Beer-bathed, rain-rinsed, reined in, past regret.
Let us, the drafted, explain nature's reign.
Drenching's more wrenching in an unbathed brain.

PICTURE

Did I take your picture?
You handed your camera to a waiter, to me.
Thereupon, you, me, and some ornaments
are stuck through eternity.

The big bar mirror behind you stationed
the booze bottles and me, too,
as the soul of your snapshot,
as though I'm kingpin of the canvas of you.

Today, I remembered you
when a picture was taken,
when flashes alerted me
to your memory awakened.

This affair keeps rankling and weighing
upon me, as a waiter and pixel arranger.
I proved careless in landscape to a dire degree,
when I anointed such scenery for you, a stranger.

Someday, someone, and *who* will know *whom*,
will look at that picture and raise a conniption.
Who is he? What a specter! And *why*
was this photographer afforded conscription?

I fear I can no longer tarry translucently traced.
I had felt as a waiter quite apart from your team.
To exist even in heaven will harbor confinement,
but to subsist common as paper is my antithetical dream.

To reside with you, over there, still pricks upon me.
For past favors, trim my mug from this digital diary,
or if erasure too monstrously muddles the scene,
tell me you ignore me. You hired me. Fire me.

TREE IN THE CITY

First, I declare no ticktock of time
tarried from the moment
I imagined the ascent
until my conquest commenced
in climbing
this municipal tree.

Long had this pine hoisted
her shaft to the clouds,
ignored, and ignoring
the construction site crowds,
as we attended
to our architectural assignments.

Up a wild vertical footpath,
I grasped hard on her limbs.
My hands battled her boughs.
Through her needles, I swam,
raking my face into red rows
of ill-matching scratches,

until I lounged near her top
and felt such ecstatic esteem.
Why am I, only I, up here, all alone?
Am I the one warrior driven to dream?

Oh, fools down below, take a chance
upon the change you have lost!

Next minute, Randy, in vanity,
a lad from the lunch truck,
climbed the tree next to mine
and began waving at me.
Then did my consonance crash.
Then did my munificence molder.

BIRDS OF COMFORT

Elation!
Gallops in alleys,
Bounds o'er the waves in the wheat,
Floats in-more out from the deep.

Sudden birds laced the ribbons
O'er my bones.
Maniacally, my flight fled,
Frantic at first, in perilous precincts.

Buoyant. Abundant. Rousing. A rhapsody
Tugging myself. And I watched me depart,
Transported in feathers, festively breezed.
I left, leaving the lost, wafting in winged luxury.

Euphoria glides. Earth simply slides.
I mean the world of before, of the hopeful
Below. Now this world nods in benignity,
Supportive of me, of the birds, of our jocosity.

When I, at last, tumbled to the turf,
No ribbon unraveled.
Only my delirium dimmed,
And the blessing burst brighter.

I lay on a corporate lawn, the landscape of the law,
Where geese waddled and ate private property grass.
They strode past me, fearless as felons,
Imagining I prey on their predators.

The geese strolled in the first snowfall of autumn.
They plodded with snow on their backs.
They condoned falling snow with such patience.
They can linger longer than snow.

Laugh into a sack.
Bag the blood of a laugh.
Oh, what we would give
To have what we have!

THIEF RIVER FALLS, MINNESOTA

Winds whisk the leaping liquid.
Gusts rake the plummeting cascade,
rummaging through the onrushing spill,
searching for swag.
No collision is heard, no correction observed.
Winds won't wiggle a waterfall, gravity's girlfriend.

The water weeps white, festooning its flight.
A dam is a wall with a pool to partition,
a bad fence but good hurdle,
a vanguard at its post,
hired to hinder the rapids.
There's room at the top if you shower.

I watched from a hospital
bordering the river,
a Thief River Falls hospital
wherein I broached birth.
I witnessed the dam
and the rebuke of the river.

A breeze brushed the brow
of the river's roof rearwards.
Upstream of the cascade,
wrinkled ripples

on the river
flowed fancifully backwards,

fleeing frantically,
ducking the dam,
creeping like a thief,
renouncing the river route,
dodging the falls,
recoiling from the roar.

Winds ruffled the scalp
of the scurrying scamp
in an upriver direction.
I fancied the breeze as a broom,
sweeping the renegade ripples,
borne back behind to the bygone.

But believe us, below,
here in the mainstream,
here by the black bottom,
the streaming is steadfast
and flows incorruptible
in the rush to the wall.

The push proceeds as a prowler,
recasting water as juice.
Do not bank on the river.

Do not swear by her course.
If she swaps her hydro for electric,
the currents are suspect.

My creamed coffee copied
the brown of the river,
the mud in the mug,
the mahogany montage.
I stirred stale cream into my coffee
with ten whirling circles.

But a cream pebble surfaced,
a rock who won't mingle,
a stone reneging enrollment.
And soon, a convocation of cream
ascended the vortex.
Floaters who want to secede.

I watched the ripples in the river
on their run from the dam.
Here in the hospital, in the riveted ruffles,
I've posed as an unshakable wave.
Today, you must be flowing away
because I've begun rolling.

NIGHT ON BOURBON STREET, NEW ORLEANS

Older than I.
Therefore, soaped in tradition.
I like this city.
I'm like this city,
a celebration in sad.

Deep doors, genially ajar, timeworn turnstiles
douse Bourbon in pink polish, in jostled jazz,
below the black and blue brows of a skyscape.
Wander the walkways in pedestrian precincts.
Stroll yesteryear's yore and history's heritage.

In the crush of the crowd,
this night blossomed into a blessing.
A riot of rain cleared Bourbon.
The soaked sightseers swarmed
under the drooled awnings.

They hid by the walls,
a hungry herd huddled in heat.
My magic sword launched, brandished, and branched.
On this night, only I bore an umbrella,
patrolling Bourbon's rainy lane alone as a godhead.

I felt their envy, their awaiting impatience,
as though I reneged on a rite, to parade
with the parasol pole, bouncing and twirling.
But I wouldn't dispatch them one drip of my street.
And I roamed in the rapport of duty neglected.

CANDLE

Fires foment infamous scandals.
Hearths harbor the most vituperative vandal.
Pyres cook, illuminate, cremate, and curtail.
Dignified, decorous, I dawned as a candle.

In an ideal world,
I wouldn't know how it feels
to flare in the world,
and not flash my ideals.

I wouldn't scorch innocent oxygen,
or whatever's my trick,
in my withering wax
on a tingling wick.

I sought not to roast.
I asked not to be florid,
nor to ignite my spirit from fibers,
nor to raise rays, then deplore it.

I fostered no choice, except to get hot.
I could prefer to chill-char my luminous leash
and blacken a frostbitten taper, if taught,
not singeing my songs from parched grease.

I begin to envision a goal in my glow,
a design for my dance,
an aim for my arching and waver,
a motive for twitching, a pretext to prance.

I hold this searing conviction
that the struggle's not ending in smolder.
If I can dip my tip into the pool, I can flee
from this shackle and conflagrate colder.

What wily bonds are weaved in my wick
that tether, fetter, tangle, and trip me
on my first step to escape,
on my jump at the galaxy?

Somehow, someway, I will writhe and contort
and scuffle and grapple, eluding the grasp.
And, by flight, end this feuding,
and, by craft, crack my manacle's clasp.

I'll brawl with the puddle,
plunging my fiery tail in her head.
We'll bicker. We'll squabble.
I kindle a conflict with thread.

And I shall lean to my left
and whirl to my right.

I'll dodge my detractors
and ascend to liberty this night.

I shall not tarry as a flame on a stick,
but as a beam bombarding through panes.
I shall spring from the ring, leap off my ledge,
and seek rods and cones of unlighted brains.

I'm thinking, *emerge*,
feeling the rips on my bonds.
I reel on the verge.
The *me* in the candle absconds.

Don't fear that my flame began drooping.
I chose to go small.
I am pouring through portholes
in the posterior wall.

CODY RODEO, WYOMING

Codeo, Codeo, Codeo, down!
From bleachers,
I am the giant who saw
drama dawn.

Here, from above, did cowboys and stallions
seem puppy cats scuffling,
given too many powers,
given too many hours.

Rider and roped, all went down laughing,
alive in the flight. Acute as a cactus.
Wraiths who ride and roll in the mud,
bewitched in the beats of their bubbling blood.

A pleasure for me to behold from afar,
another way of it all, a gala for ghosts,
as though I might escape through any corral,
though fences feel friendly on my side of the posts.

Years later, I remembered the cowboys of Cody,
a little, but one I remember as regal:
the one who sat still on a huge horse by the exit.
He made rodeo normal, wholesome, and legal.

It's one thing to go hand-in-hoof dancing a jig,
but in life and in rodeo, the last horse is big.

SECRETS

A secret is a parcel strung
with gender dependence.
I say two sexes of secrets sequester.

See-crets and say-crets
wander the world.
A man loads a secret

on the bridge of his back.
It parks most obvious there,
but it sojourns secure.

A man totes a simmering secret
to augment his disguise,
feeling the flush

of the furtive,
the mask of the mystic,
where a tale tarries in solitude.

A man imprisons this imp in his mind,
knowing the storm is inside,
knowing the unknown.

A man thinks a secret seeks his protection,
and a man glares back at a thief
who would snatch the flag from its mast.

A man and a secret convene the occult,
the comfortable clouds,
the classified.

A woman slants the slope of a secret,
knows which secrets teem with tempers,
knows which secrets fit in a fib.

A woman's secret is stowed in a hose.
She spills a splash on the flower,
but keeps flicking the nozzle.

A woman fancies her secret a roommate
and introduces her bunkmate
to bedfellows.

A woman and a secret share marrow.
Both are privileged and strange.
Both lay latent.

A woman half trusts a secret
to slide under the door,
to another side.

ODE TO GRAVITY

Almighty Tipper!
> Thou who rolled the egg to crack
In thy feral frolic, Gravity.
> Thou grant grits a grip upon gravy
And hide holes in the cosmos
> To gather light into black.
Thy battalion bully and bulldoze,
> Not battle in bravery,
Thou who tow the pendulum
> And pluck the hourglass sand,
And coax the somnolent slumber
> Of the hovering snow,
And catch rolling dice on the table,
> And snare goldfish in a bowl.
Thy hand ladles soup in the seas
> And secures souls on dry land.
Thy tides teeter, arising to flow,
> And, when fallen, lie low.
We fail in our flights, humbled,
> Tumbled, for thus is thy role.

Grim Gravity! Solemn purveyor
> Of every graviton grain,
Thou hast gussied up galaxies
> But left trash in our dump.

Thou reigned o'er drizzle's descent
    And the drop to the drain.
Thou limited the luck of our leaps,
    Binding the bounds of each jump.
Thou mustered workaday coordinates
    In each methodical orbit.
Faster, faster, thou forced
    An acceleration to nowhere.
The popcorn pops up.
    The popcorn lies down.
Surely, each ceiling now dangles
    For thee to then floor it.
No creature dodges thy clutches,
    Nor flies free from thy snare,
Till that hour when princely Power
    Snatches thy crown.

Cheerless Gravity!
    Earnest and sincere in thy meddling,
Thou decree my attraction
    For the rocks 'neath my feet.
Thou ordain my old orb to maneuver
    The moon into settling
Closer to me, though yet on the outskirts,
    Not the same street.
Legends allege that even *I* pester
    Our patrol round the sun

Because of *my* meager mass.
    Yet a galaxy's gallop guards our gap,
Not as my mission, not due to my appeal,
    Allure, or rare grace.
I muster a mass of marbles, an item,
    A trinket, a token, just one,
A bump on a boundless boulevard,
    A scrap on the map.
But in the face of spectacular space,
    I can't erase thine embrace.

Gravity grinds in spasmodic measures,
    To wrench torpor from twitch,
To wrest languorous loiter
    From the launch of commotion,
Calming the confetti, bowing the baseball,
    Placating each pitch,
Plying thy potion, tethering trees upon turf,
    Sealing surf in the ocean,
Obliging raucous rockslides to dive,
    Charming the swarming lava to sink.
Thou hast dignity, somber Gravity,
    Conjuring each capsizing and spilling,
But thy prestige is meager, thy demeanor
    Too eager to render thee renown.
Thou art but a seducer to lure, pluck,
    And yank, not gifted to think

Upon thy fate as a puller, not the pusher
> Of the pulse in hearts of the willing.
Lower me to my grave, O Gravity,
> But hark! I'll ne'er again step down.

APRIL GOOSE

Through my basement library window,
a goose sat under my bush,
biting her body to feather a nest.
Her meandering neck,
milky white, pecked plumes
from her frame. She's a bearded belle.
Her beak nibbled like scissors,
before belle babes are born.
Eggs were over easy.
Hatching was underway hard.

A gander, too, gawked at me
through my library window,
tapping the glass with his beak,
seeing himself, a rival reflected
in the ghostly goose glass.
His taunting tongue crept from its cradle.
He tapped against the trenchant intruder
harbored near his home, hereabouts,
till I tapped back.
Then he tapped against sinister sidekicks.

My nose nuzzled the glass, and I gazed,
reckless, resolute, recalcitrant,
until he hoisted his head

to immerse me in a rational eye.
Perhaps he marked me as thunder,
as he fanned his wing to extinguish it.
Maybe I seemed a deity hoisting the heavens,
a wizard wandering the nether terrain.
Maybe I epitomized the Creator's compulsion,
or manifested the mayhem muddling his mind.

I gaped into his beak's nostrils,
black sacks in the abyss. Sharp ovals
encased this boulevard's boundary.
His eyelid ascended, floating
a pearly button to behold me.
Then his eyelid slammed shut,
overturned without tumult.
He rested—as if
I were a soft danger, a dim menace,
a companion.

LOVE LETTER
(GHOSTWRITER GIVEAWAY)

My dearest Girl,

Two minds meet.
Two brains bubble

sauce in our spaghetti,
nerves in our noodles.

I write this in front
of bounces ahead.

My trust tumbled upon you.
I launched into love.

I post pure exposure.
I will affirm fiery faith

till you contrive a conviction to empty
this milieu moored amidst me,

till your vortex vacates every vestige,
and your verdicts vesture the verse of my void.

I forgo fond frontiers,
forgathering faith in my fortune.

Love,
[Insert digitized signature. Click OK.]

ALLIS & JOHN & TRACTOR TRACKS

She wasn't Allis without John.
I have known a neighbor
and schoolmate to show change
in behavior when a husband
is long absent or a wife's out of range.

John Deere was my comrade in mowing,
after Allis reaped our Spring sowing.
Allis Chalmers and I combed the field
when John's sickle stripped the stems naked.
I straddled Allis so Allis could rake it.

I knew each blemish and odor of Allis.
I recount the bounce of my balls
upon her seat cushion
as we rolled over a gopher mound,
or down an old bison wallow

and over big roots.
Her steering wheel buzzed
in my hands to my boots.
Her aloft smoke pipe was attached
to a latched cover on top

that fluttered open and closed without stop,
but with small pauses that seemed a flirtation.
Her hot pipe hovered so near to my face,
with her capped chomping oyster atop,
fuming each flop.

She talked some to me with her veiled vixen voice.
She laughed a lot at her jockey, a nonchalant noise.
But she moaned when I bounced her,
and she screamed once when her belt pulley broke,
but I fixed it right there in the smoldering smoke.

Her big rear wheels were monstrously mine.
To left, to right, they resolved to revolve.
I flew on a Ferris wheel,
so it seemed to me, sometimes,
around and around.

I can't conceive I controlled her.
She sought an adventure,
not the harvest that rolled her.
I rode her so steady till I'd forgotten my place
in the fields, daydreaming I'm running a race,

without conjuring the cast of that space,
until I took her through the slope by the river,
then slowed her plenty,
and let her set the pace,
so she'd not overturn on my face.

I could go nine or ten hours on Allis.
I want to finish a chore, only then I enjoy rest.
I rode a brash breeze on a farm field at dawn.
Those gusts withdraw if you're walking,
but I knew the wild wind atop

orange Allis and green John. Ever,
I parked Allis by the house, so I'd see her
through my window. I set her in profile
to witness those powerful thighs,
and the grease on her breast,

and her tracks in the ruts,
and the itch and the urge
and wish and will in her guts.
I can tell you she was pretty in the rain,
and she was the belle of a meadow in glory.

She was modest, perhaps,
but discernably vain.
Allis and I will grow old apart,
still smelling like grain,
still good for used parts, and a part allegory.

Many a man gets bewitched
by his benefactor,
but now I can't fathom one day

when my reveries lacked her.
At last, I couldn't take it no more,

and my lips finally smacked her,
and I ain't saying no more,
ain't saying I packed her.
Just saying, lackluster love limps,
unless you've loved a tractor.

I can't tattle no tales about John.
Him and me hit it off,
teammates for a short bloom.
We're friends, but professional.
Ain't aiming to lengthen my time

at confessional.
Ain't aiming to suffer more hours
in a courtroom.
But if you ever see Allis in her glory,
when I'm not around her, see if you

can do even more to astound her.
Pull her throttle and choke.
I ain't jealous, don't worry.
You'll be the next lucky bloke
to sow this same, same old story.

SWINGING OVER LA JOLLA SHORES

I can depict the diameter of Daylight to Dark
from my spree on the Shores of La Jolla,
on the cusp of California's blue brine.

Daylight on the Shores beguiles the idle,
the idle who walk half naked by day,
the idle who herd with the idle.

Think! What a hymn I would hatch on this shore,
but for the burden of these opulent poor.
Let me and the sun clear this floor.

She in the west spilt swift sizzling rust. Sunset
squeezed into the ocean, her Pacific hotel room,
for one night only—smoking; shared bath.

Now, the moon whetted my whimsy for mischief.
The idle are gone from the shores.
I and their absence bequeathed a blithe blessing

to sanction the sanctity of one soul in the dark.
To the swings!
To my seat suspended by chains,

to hurly-burly, hilarity, hullabaloo,
to arc to-and-fro and to peculiarize
the heavier half of a circle.

Swing into the smell of salt vapor.
Swing out of the hampering herd.
Swing up to the beckoning stars.

I spied my spot in tenantless space,
swinging back windy
from the summoning surf.

I ceased pushing my feet,
as the swooshing surf rocked me back,
and the stampeding stars rolled me up.

O how these seconds ensnared me!
O magnetized moment a memory was birthed!
O to snatch bliss from the black!

Wondrous wilds whittled my wits.
In liberty, I leapt, launching alive,
swinging over the sea.

What motive for I in the telling
to you of my moment,
my glorious moment of life?

No, I think not to elicit your envy.
Yes, I think rather to spill over the lid.
Though, I think chiefly to summon recall

of that one memory of yours,
the night you swung over the sea
and failed to tell me.

MOON LANDING

Upon their moon landing, canned men thought
the thought of Magellan, the thought of Balboa:
"I may now be possibly here!"
Go onwards, as directed,
and look how lovely was there.

There are three sorts of explorers,
to my way of thought:
one I love to their marrow,
one I cultivate,
one I jealously hate.

The inventor
ranks first among men,
for I love Nature's subversion
and the ignition
of minds.

The discoverer
rates as our inquisitive peer,
one who searches for peas
or cucumbers,
but spots apples, by blunders.

    The adventurer
roosts as a newly hatched eaglet,
who bullies the nest,
pecking his siblings.
They fall so that he may fly.

On each voyage, on sails or on silicon,
find the adventurer, the one
with the itchy anus,
and the stinking scalp,
who leverages luck and local largesse.

Whether the Holy Grail,
the White Whale,
the New World,
the Flying Dutchman,
find a poser in the poster.

"We will unlock," says the inventor
(interviews; measured).

"We will look," says the discoverer
(reviews; mesh erred).

"I will see," says the adventurer
(views; me assured).

AUKTOBOR WINT

Wint, this hour,
tousles and tumbles.
Wist of cloud
swarls near to world.
Leaf leaves,

rupping in rags.
Fronds flake, fly,
torn in tufts.
Wint hoists hair
off our scalps.

A leaf is but a bird
to the wint.
A flock, a flurry,
big hurry,
waves through grass.

I spy a pantomimist approaching.
A laughing tree,
near blown to its heels,
dozen arms waving round
to right itself.

The tree laughs and laughs,
waves arms to catch its stance,
waves arms to wink at the wint,
arms in nature play,
arms in the festival.

Though we must be dying,
we can't stop laughing.
Wint, wint, push me again and again.
Maybe rain arrives, exhales in this hour,
but wint inhales the roar and the pour.

PUNTING ON THE RIVER CAM, CAMBRIDGE, UK

I cast off from Quayside,
where punters accrue,
to float as a freeloader
on the calm River Cam.
I've greased this green water
till my toil oiled it anew.
From the strokes of my quant,
the Cam knows what I am.

I've poled a flatboat when Cam
gleamed green from the lawns.
My pole sloshed through the stream,
digging holes in the mud,
and guarding my sandwich
from the thieving, tame swans.
I can still fork over false folklore.
I've got yesteryear in my blood.

I poled as a River Cam tour guide
till pulling my life's worst mistake,
when I tried to school a girl rider
on gripping and grappling the pole.
Lithe lassie, poke the pole downward,
but lead it out straight as a rake,

then drag the pole like a rudder,
like it renders a steering wheel role.

When the pole stuck in the mud,
she flew overboard bound,
and the punt hadn't a paddle,
hadn't a swimmer, hadn't a brake.
And that lassie was drowned.
And that lass was renowned.
And that lass was the last
my punt would ever forsake.

Now I punt alone, just to hear
the splash and the swish,
when my poling digs whispers
from the wind and the water,
as though I were debating a duck,
as though I were quizzing a fish.
But I keep trawling the stream, alas,
for a lost lassie. Forever, I sought her

where overhung willow trees dip
their fingertips into the Cam
and strike musical memories
of remembrance and ruin,
of every progenitor's progeny,
of every forefather's grandam.

The Cam harbors harsh history
and trickles the tracks of its tune.

I punt past ancient Cambridge,
college libraries and churches,
where scholars and philosophers
taught in stone mansions.
Tourists add King's, Clare, Trinity,
and St John's in their searches,
but no one remembers
us outcasts in the stanchions.

The Cam creeps in a crawl, and I've strived
to pole myself back upstream of her story,
but time keeps escaping, and I'll never race
to reverse my abominable blunder.
Like water in winter, these college halls froze
as brick boxes, arresting time and its glory.
But an apparition keeps pulsing, an allure
of the long-ago lost that awakens our wonder.

On River Cam, the best punting path
runs smack down the center,
where stones from an old roadway
still convene to carpet the floor.
St John's stones rise up from the river,
but not the side that you enter,

unless your wit's in your wishes
and your desire's a door.

Cam glides under stone bridges,
whose arches ogle like eyes.
And before gaining the gaze
of the Mathematical Bridge,
my sentiments surfaced asunder,
under the oft-crossed Bridge of Sighs,
where I spied a pub on the docks,
beckoning by a daffodil ridge.

I hoisted a pint of potent pale ale,
perhaps a pint poured fresh from the Cam,
dipped and drawn as a chalice of time,
as a brimming beaker of river that ran.
I dallied in draining my draft, reckoning
this river rightfully knows what I am—
a ruffle to wrinkle the run of the Cam,
a ripple that passes and comes not again.

ORCHESTRAL RAIN

A hollow night harbored
the splashing of heaven.
The rain rallied the summer
and placed me in its plot,

in the hymn through my window.
Celestial symphonics descended,
a nimbus cloud orchestra,
entire, intact, a roll call of rain.

A silent whistle, a raindrop,
played for her patrons,
sent as a heaven-born herald,
a song authored in the ether.

A tuneful puddle in grass,
a flask filled up with flutes,
pooled its piccolo peeps
from teardrops tapping the bongos.

Ripped from the roof of our realm,
horns, strings, and drums plummeted.
The rain percussed as a rumor,
trumpeting a galaxy's gossip.

In absent thunder, in tardy bolts,
a subtle Composer creates
climactic moments
from hushed histrionics.

Scherzo sounds wet.
Rondo ricochets.
Each player plucks once,
but what a grand band!

All raindrops, all rascals,
toot one note and then vanish,
but find a harmonious chord
in the splats of the horde.

SPRING COVENANT

In this cattle pasture, a ravine rambled,
a ladle for rainfall, when her mudbanks
are softest in Spring.
Reveries sank into her traveling tank,
cold to my fingers, as I scooped
the wild water from the ravine into my jar
and apprized frisky floaters in frolic,
now near, from afar.

My plunder of Nature that day
was only beginning.
My gaze appraised a leaf,
its stem frozen to grass,
with its hand wildly waving
in a reckless wind's urging.
I stole the winter's red leaf,
in ice nearly liquid, nearly gas.

One feels more like a robber
when abducting a stone,
which I pulled from the pasture,
where this scarred rock lay alone.
I gripped it tight in my fist
until I pulled the cold from its heart.
One rock indivisible,
until its stones drift apart.

Displayed on my mantel,
these wild of Nature lost
none of themselves,
lost none of the Nature they crossed,
in resting instead on my altar to Nature,
loved by this boy,
as pawns that he'd pushed,
as knights that he'd shoved.

Indeed, Nature sprang sprightly
in its debut on my dais.
The stone seemed a lighter, hard weight,
a reachable star. And the leaf
now etched the presence of absence,
the shocking of wonder.
See the tamed larvae jackknifing,
the selfsame in a sea or a jar.

Now in my nest,
they splashed more tattles for me.
Why then did I next day return them,
feral and free,
and place in the pasture
the stone back in its imprint,
and set the leaf upon the ice
under a motherly tree?

And from the jar, the wild water I poured
gently to the last liquid lap
into the ravine,
whence she was doubtless last seen.
Or at least her new neighbors
suffused an acquaintance,
melted her in with merely a handshake
and a tip of the cap.

What is this farthest world
whose furnishings tempt me?
What dearer world do I alone fill
and I aloof empty!

CROSSING

Across all the years of stopping here,
my journey ends,
your pond begins.
My neighbor's water rights are clear.

But today, my steps crossed the edge's end,
heedlessly and needlessly.
On this frigid day, the pond was iced.
Snow entombed the border's bend.

If I were heaven's keeper, sojourning as a swan,
I wouldn't give this pond one feather.
But heaven sowed her snow this day
in fresh frontiers, with bolder borders drawn.

I stepped upon its ice, still stiff below the snow.
I started and could not stop my stalking
across the pond, though, whether crossing
its breadth or depth, I would come to know.

The rub of boots kept rasping louder.
The grunt of ice forecast my bath
below a path I trusted, below a track unseen,
below the carpet of cold white powder.

The path ahead avowed its pavement.
Wee weight for her, I'm dainty cargo.
Unaware of me, she'd lift her roof.
But will she tuck me in her basement?

Snowfall surged and sought to sift
and sieve me through her blustery screen.
I stepped, I stepped across her curtains,
a soul among the swirling drift.

I forgot my frigid feet kept walking.
Each step delved deeper and dissolved
in my flight, flown with a daft propeller.
My gait steered straight. My heart kept knocking.

Sacred snow of heaven hovered
and fostered frosty tears upon my face.
I stood alone, the central pier upon a pond,
at last discovered, my life uncovered.

For years, I'd hoped to walk away.
Now, at last, I'd act upon my wish,
to flee, forsake, forget, forswear.
I believed—it is this day.

Then I stepped upon my neighbor's shore.
The ghostly storm had blown behind,

to fade at docks of my departure, tossed in time,
till tomorrow's tempests dally at my door.

I discerned the crunch of footfalls nearing.
I divined a rare halloo
and thought how, unsought,
the crossing brought a clearing.

TROMBONE SOCIETY

My tailor's report:
your right arm registers an inch
longer than the left.
You must have played
the trombone.

He matched the coat to the man
with a measure.
Might an appendage's span
tattle the tale of a man,

just as the surge of the slither
and the sail of the slide
report the purport of the players
of trombone?

A honking haven and hypnotic harbor
slides through the glides
of trombone.

Who judges the journey, to one jot,
of each jump along its piston, pulsating
at the end of every run?
Who knows, to one spout and one spot,
the spoons of sap that spat
from the trombonist's spewing spit?

A rim of red semicircle resides
over the lip of trombone players.
The trombonist minds his machinery.
The audience minds his industry.

Trombones hover everywhere,
hereby humble, hereby haughty,
voicing vanity to violins, feeling natty,
sounding blatty, but perpetually mobile,
slippery, slick, and imperiously noble.
A trombone, when blown, seems overgrown,
a horn born to grumble, howl, and cackle,
a horn summoned to the brawl,
to bruise, to brood, to leap when clarinets crawl.

One never plays trombone truly.
Not so much is demanded, and so,
therein lies the heart's slide.
To be forever the blusterous blowhard
who failed with passion and pride:
the impossible horn who tried.

There are no friends
in trombone society,
only the guileful and guilty,
who, at times, breathe together.

THE MILLYROO SONG

What if an emotion could last
and live in the place where it felt?
When would its motion flow past?
How would the emission be smelt?
Millyroo, millyroo, millyroo ray.

Chumps and champions suffer the same:
the spotlight sprays us with a scoop from the sky
to festoon our foibles in God's glamorous game.
The insane things that happen beguile the Big Guy.
'Ray, Milly, 'ray, Milly, 'ray millyroo ray.

Every temptation and vice sat on my table to sniff.
How will I choose, and what choice did it seem?
Was my choosing a chosen? I still wonder if
the chosen choose wisely for chosen esteem.
Oh, millyroo-oh. Oh, millyroo ray.

Bravery is nothing but malfunctioning thought
on the briefness of life.
If ten million years could be bought,
stay home in your armor, in the arms of the wife.
Roo, millyroo, too. Roo, millyroo ray.

All decent people are passive-aggressive.

All recent actions arise in the right way,
uncertain in precepts, but certainly festive.
Universal expansion led local expression astray.
Milly and Milly and millyroo ray.

Every rogue and rapscallion and rascal at play
still loves a good singing.
I wish for one people, one planet, one way.
I wish for extinctions in parts of our kingdom.
Millyroo, millyroo, millyroo ray.

VACUUM PUMP

Parts list! This pump pixie
boasts its beguiling insignia,
proclaims its pucker propagated
from her plain sisters
in the owner's manual:
installation, operation, and maintenance.

Try a gaze through the gauze of our heavens.
It's quiet and clean in the vacuous cosmos.
Maybe two vanes of a rotating rotor roost
eccentrically mounted in a space-time ring
on a common shaft. The Divine Realm is driven
through severe inhalation. Air-cooled, oil sealed.

Oil is supplied to all moving parts to quell friction
and cool fevers with heat dissipation.
In vented exhaust, in a hushed rush, gusts puff.
Luscious lubrication and a sealed virtuous vacuum
launch the grand evacuation
that extends over the stars.

Just so, I employed my petite pumper to dry
a vessel I had labeled as wet.
I dried this chamber to vacuity,
drained to exhaustion and absence,

swept to nothingness, quite depleted and blank,
tenantless, free, and deserted.

Audaciously, I ousted an atmosphere.
My pump squeezed and rippled its nipples.
My pump pinched its greased gaskets.
And I held as a newborn,
for a time ticketed as mine,
my tiny and beautiful void.

FALLEN

The stream falling from my faucet
takes only one path:
it completely ignores me.
It has someplace to go.
It's in a hurry
to reach one special spot
ahead of the next.

I falter at falling.
At first, I felt fooled into falling.
Then, failing falling,
there followed a feeling
of standing.
Though the stars traipse as travelers,
they pass me unflapping.

I find that I've fallen alone.
It's a blessing.
I know puddles and weeds
never known.
I know the work of my hands
on some tumbledown trifles
that I alone know.

I pursued while I fell
a personal interest
in protecting my things,
for my private posterity.
I fostered a focus
on grasping my gains, apart
from your advice and consent.

In each age of Mankind,
the fallen have known
an underlayer of knowing,
not told, not transcribed.
The fallen choose to preserve
history's precious pith in a pouch.
Historians hoist the drips of the nectar.

REPLACEMENTS

An overmuch and lavish
log out,
a supple sausage,
to tincture my sphincter.

The parting was a pleasure.
We divided none from ill will,
and the coarse crossing chorus
yet crowed in affection.

From my cup to my colon,
I felt the better in empty,
though I pined for the departed,
and sought palatable replacements.

Try the beef stew over noodles
at Buzzy's Saloon.
Try it for the thrill at the threshold
of its intestinal adventure.

Relish its arrival in the lobby
of the tumbling tunnel.
Savor smooches and pecks on the porch
of the plummeting pipeline.

Just so, I greet grog and grant gravy
for Nature's untidy tongue.
She will sigh high when I'm relishing,
enrolling, and relinquishing my tasty replacements.

SPIDER & FLY & I

Ponder a tailor everyone knows,
now outside my window,
once more sewing her screen.
A bee bounced off the net
and tore tatters of trampoline.
The next guest looked like an angel,
a flying green worm with webbed wings,

an angel tressed to entangle
and sit sewn by the tailor.
The spider wrapped ribbons
around the grievous, green groceries.
A second green angel, her mate,
I surmised, hovered over the net,
trembling in air, with indissoluble care,

puzzled that her mate slept with a neighbor.
She sought to unwrap our realm's riddle.
She seemed to solicit my counsel.
"Do you know——?"
"No."
I spoke this one word aloud,
fearing the angel and I might fancy to fly.

THE ROT SHE WROUGHT

Walking, stalking, talking loud,
bombarding us with expiration,
she spat her spit, begat a cloud,
spouting from her sordid station.

She launched her laugh,
propelled her plagues,
never knew the half
of the blokes she granted graves.

Venting virus to the void she fostered,
Pandemic Piper, source of sickness.
None would know the obits she authored.
She slew with adventitious wickedness,

scattered scourge to spill her ills.
Soon her friends fell, fraught with ailing.
Fevers festered, instilled with chills.
Palliative care when drugs kept failing.

Milady malady, font of affliction,
queen of carnage, pandemic princess,
roosts outside our jurisdiction,
though we segregate by only inches.

Piper feigns, defames us all as falsifiers.
The source of the virus must ne'er be found.
She leads elites, a choir of liars,
royal rogues, renounced, renowned.

COUNTY CARNIVAL

Foretaste her, the county carnival,
a mile ahead along the road.
Hear the happy machine.
See the falling rim of rained bow.

Smell animal candy.
A mile past, and I
am exposed as the new
main attraction

for all beasts and all blasts.
Here, air's ruffles expand.
Here, effluvium floats,
and lights are fresh from the oven.

She slackened her clutch on my collar
to stir me less,
to stir him more, he, a mile thence,
whence her whisper summoned another.

ADAM & EVE,
ACCORDING TO STEVE

Cherish the last merry moments
of man, any man,
in the beginning
of Adam.

Relish silence.
Savor serenity.
Fete the freedom from lust
when dust dangled distinctly male dust.

If Steve could reclaim Adam's lost rib,
or if only Eve had more artfully hid,
of his wife, he'd be rid.
We'd all avert the slow skid

from what Eve callously did
to hatch the next kid
and intern men amid
Girl World 'neath her lid.

In the beginning, no man,
no Adam, then lacked it:
the peace of one forward step
and a second that backed it.

But God loves a gal
and can't love the alone,
the alone that men love.
Men love a calm home.

God saw in His head
Steve, not now all alone,
and He said in His head,
It is good.

The plan in His head
worked like a charm.
Man kept womanhood warm,
free from alarm, sequestered from harm.

God draped daylight with Eve
and yanked Adam from shade,
so lovers could weave,
so others got made.

The plan freed Eve from alone, only.
For Steve, the plan perpetuates lonely.

GRADUATION SPEAKER FOR HIRE
(HAVE DRAFT — WILL TRAVEL)

eschew anonymous service,
raise a rumpus with trumpets,

catapulting your cachet,
parading your patronage,

but proclaim a prompt payment
as a salute to your assistance.

bankroll the bursar,
and clandestinely curse her.

no, wait! i've caroled the wrong chorus
for our throng of the righteously wrong.

i've finally pocketed my wage.
hence, i'll divulge the next page.

children, renounce
the glamor of virtue.

do not, with panache,
brush me crumbs from your table.

no fine feat of the one
may be attained by the collective.

on this, your last day in school,
neglect this trite trip.

defer the flat hat
and black frock

until you loaf in your burial box
on your day of graduation.

HEAVEN

Do not call me in heaven
to ask what I meant.
Do not worry eternity
with your inquiry.

Do not call me in heaven
to ask where it is.
You're sure to find it
if you seek it and mind it.

If things go as planned,
I aim to be busy
in sleeping a fancy
and waking a memory.

In case of emergency,
leap to my location.
Or if it seems better,
write me a letter.

NEW TOWNS

I come upon no new towns anymore.
My old, old map is current
and up-to-date
with all the towns.

According to fish,
land is the boundary.
Land confines.

Some new roads sprout in old towns,
roads recoiling from towns,
but not enough.

I will be down indirectly.

I'm new too.
Did you wipe your sandals?
No matter,
I'm changing the pavement.

I'm touring my tidewater town
as a crack in the girders.
I flip water.

Passed you
a drip.

Missed the bucket.

PROGRESSIVE CAT

My cat can hesitate,
hoisting sharp thoughts,
betwixt three steps on the rug
and her next neck rotation.

For a reason as random as that, I asked it.
Do I have a progressive cat?
The sort who would start
a party of one and some?

Birth panics progress. Death puckers progress.
Progress propels a series, a sequence, a sequel.
Progress splats neither bad nor good,
unlike cancer and ketchup. It spews only progress.

Supposing that a man
could prize himself progressive
and hide his humiliation
by throwing a party,

I sat on that day a-wondering
whether my cat is quixotic.
One paw on my collarbone,
she's tasting my chin.

She counts the claws on her lax paw,
and my eyes evade her stern gaze.
I've believed with some satisfaction
I please her with intellect, not affectation.

But her face is of a kind
that accuses a liar.
She ain't saying if she's progressive,
but before reaching roll call in the catacombs,

she hoped for a remarkable question.

WHO

Ask Maxine who I am.
Polite but shy.
Ask Deborah who.
Arrogant, why?

Tom sought my thinking.
Kate caught me drinking.
To Barbara, I'm pensive.
To Mark, I'm defensive.

I was pious for him,
in the morning.
I was playful for her,
in the end.
I will say and seem anything
to avoid a next moment
with them.

In all my life,
I have never
invited myself to tag along,
conspicuously.

We prefer to be by myself.
We whittle our whereabouts,
but we keep our appointments.

THE FORTY-NINTH GRAVE

In forty-nine purchasable graves
lay forty-eight Lutherans.
The cemetery slept near our farms.
A boy I was then,
when mowing graves warms
a farmer boy's chest,
thinkin' *I'm only a guest.*
For I'm only a guest.

Now I'm fifty years more,
and all my neighbors took graves.
Only God knows the grounds
why it's my rump He saves,
to stand here again,
alive among the dead,
to nearly regret and partway deplore
the life that I led.

Why'd I 'splain death to you?
You've suffered the seizure of grieving
while squirting tears here
among those in quietest leisure.
It'd jigger the town's sniggers
if my skeleton parked boxed and in storage,
but when here it's me all who's left—
hee, it can sand a town's courage.

But ye sleepers below, give some pity for me,
me, here a-meltin' in yer late summer heat.
I promised the departed I'd stay till sun setting,
and it's my full word that they're getting.

Ain't no high-trafficked road
rimmin' this holiest field.
I saw only Kempinski
and his horses pass now. And he
probably snickered 'bout how long it'd be
afore I'm a-gonna foller
back to the shadow,
back to my boozin' and smokin' and waller

and the scalable calm
of Hennie's beer parlor.
Say now, after the sun sets,
it ain't nearly so warm to the toes!
But that ain't the cardinal point.
I don't like this top
to the bottom of night—
not while straddlin' these rows.

It's not like me to teeter
nor pause weighing a totter,
but it's me here that's wiping
his face full of water.

That surging of shadows—
at first, it's all me—
next moment, it's all of them names
and dates that I see.

Afore sunrise, I'll hand-wipe
forty-eight headstones,
with only my glowin' smokepipe
for yard light,
and furnish a fresh 'quaintance
with a million muh-skeeters,
given a free and fresh chance to nibble
on me and the night,

me, the town's titled "deadbeat and grafter,"
when not titled the "drunken him-fer-example."
When they're expectin' to smell yuh by sight,
yer the life of their laughter.

But with my headstone scrubbing and cleaning,
I'm scheming
to pilfer a purchase of the forty-ninth grave,
just so, for me, it gits saved.

First on my calling is the late Miss Lallian Denke,
who lifetimes was hintin' I needed a bath.
Let's get a committee. Let's get a court rulin',
and likewise, summon a rater of vapor with schoolin',

'n' get a new-matic compressor
with the barrel and gauge.
Let's grade your smell force to mine
now and don't trim the math.
I'll wager Lallian's stench soars
o'er any skunk who would mate her,
o'er any polecat who'd date her,
and by the ton that I hate her.

It goes good while yer cussing
'n' lettin' them have it,
but for that sudden quick smack
of the quietness back.

Next on my monument stops
is the late Sami L. Neilsson,
yes, the famous one—Ha!
Always towards me, he was stoopin',
like he's scoldin' a dog.
Always towards me, like he's slopping a hog.
Always towards me, like he's down-talkin'
from the second-floor privy.

But I once see'd the quakin' scare in his scowl
from my half of his lumberjack's saw.
Him like the clock that goes ticking
till he hears my tock and goes quivery.

And here lies his missus to boot, ol' Ruth,
always sayin' to me t' stay 'way from her girls,
as if seein' my carcass could confuse li'l Mollie
as she's hand-feedin' her squirrels.

For a minute, I glower
at the boneyard's one leafy oak tower.
It's so 'posing and 'portant
like the blab of a rooster,
like yer lucky location
and yer high-handed height
and yer chance solitude
grants yuh a say-so to power.

My knee balls keep crackin'
from bendin' to stone after stone,
but I'm not sure to thinkin'
'bout walking back home,
with sparkin' tobacco
as a blood moon's twin lantern,
with too much time to be ponderin'
if I'd reap what I'd sown.

And though it'll take hours, I keep on my pledges
to clean forty-eight names on forty-eight edges.
I'll spit shine each marker with the tail of my shirt
and claw out the etches onto my fingernail dirt.

On her grave hump, I stammer,
Lois Cowhead Stolynnia,
the foe of my fortune.
And though I wernt her killer,
the town hens sure wondered
why, after our fightin',
she starts gettin' iller
and iller.

By her talkin' and squawkin',
the whole county knew
'bout them eggs.
I stole nine from her hen herd,
and I could scream that I'd done it.
It ruined my meek name
and slapped shed paint through my portrait,
and I walk life in shame.

I see it like Sunday—
I petted them chickens like puppies
and reached through their legs,
and their nest felt so warm.
My hand lingered a while,
and when I pulled out my paw,
it's a marvel and blessing I saw.
I bagged a bucket of eggs.

Wernt even no henhouse,
just birthin' in brush.
Those eggs were as sturdy as stones.
Never even wanted to fry 'em
or scramble their guts.
Saw 'em winkin' and shinin' like bones,
and they warmed through my hand.
Their shells shimmered and shone.

I cradled all nine in the stretch of my sweater.
I hid 'em like diamonds
under the gloves in my toolbox,
'n' kept peekin' like I laid 'em my own.

It was Lars, now lying here,
who found 'em while snoopin' around,
and he gives Cowhead
a fine sing.
If then my fondest wish
were to slide further to nothing,
then my life got the better,
for I was the impaled bull in the ring.

That thinkin' provokes me to walk 'cross
this throng to where Dagmar's chain-napping,
and, God tell me, not dreamin' of me.
My stealin' his garden taters was wrong.

I tell so you know it. I sold 'em to Schumm,
almost a-grinnin'.
Yeah, I got the money,
but I did it for fun.
Told Dagmar, *Yer perfectly right
and I'm wrong,*
while his spuds sit under my hat,
so in the end, I'm still winnin'.

I recall that one blizzard at midnight
while I'm wiping Parmalee's stone.
Him pounding on my door
as I lay drunk on my floor.
Never did tell him
whether that night I was at home.
Never did ask him
what all that fierce poundin' was for.

Never hearda no crisis concernin' him or the wife,
nor asked his reasons nor mine
for the lost hello and goodbye.
Never asked them their reasons to die.

Kekkonin's marker took the slant of the man,
and I'm still here leanin' to please him.
So, I still hear his horse team and feel the slide
of the plow from a half summer season.

You see, for those folks in the field,
it's like an obsession,
them wrasslin' wheat from a chaff.
I'll plow dirt as tame as an ox if you
cough up those coins on my payday.
But that night, I jimmied the locks,
and I added my coins to the ones
I stole from your box.

Big Kekkonin knows all,
all under the cap of the heaven,
'cept what he don't know
about anything past.
I spent shrewdly my June earnings
on keg beer 'n' skirts,
refusin' to lose it
on laughs.

"Can I have this dance?"
I said this to Carol McKennicot's granite—
who else!
I'll spill the story 'bout Carol,
the hall, and the feet,
and the one-step
or two-step,
with Carol's direction and beat.

After we voted her "events" director
at the township hall, Carol
set down twelve paper-made footprints,
six marked left and six right,
to direct the marchin'
to tangos and waltz.
It was so perfect to peculiar,
we started aping a ball.

To this day, I go half hopin' to see
these pilotin' footprints before me appear.
A man might not go far wrong
when those footprints usher and steer.
When the town cop pulls up beside me,
those footpaths could run off and hide me.
Only you know, like me,
we'd spend the rest o' a lifetime

tryin' to slide them. In fact,
I didn't much like Carol's plan-ahead layout.
For all o' our dancin' ends in a circle.
Dancin' don't let troubles and tragedy play out.

Off left are the Hanes's graves.
They all spoke nice to me,
not affection,
but some like a strategy.

Sir, if you can trow what a Hanes
is true thinkin',
yer a-better than a Hanes
or than me.

I'd count eleven
that once were Bachmanns,
who now sleep
in their interminable grass hole,
more palatial than their pigsty
parking back home.
And, hey, here's Becky,
who kissed that lamb that I stole.

I'd want to pass over
the hard feelin's of Jansson.
He sure loved that dog that I poisoned.
But boy! He was a snapper
and wunt share me the road,
and it's my own
dainty twinned stragglers
that by his snout were too moistened.

My first-round visits
passed as personal,
but it's to their full assembly
I'm ponderin' my lecture.

Just for but a minute or two,
not like dead Milly here,
nor like ol' Erno
and his gallopin' conjecture.

While aspen trees rattle, I speak loudly my piece,
in a heart-to-heart handed to the forty-eight 'ceased:
"Ain't the guest you'd expected to run out the rounds
and bow humble my body at the boot of your mounds.

"We're some reacquainted,
'n' say for most it maybe ain't no delight.
I recollect Katrina here would tell me,
Renounce the runway of wrong over right.
There're two kinds of people,
one catches, one kicks it.
There're them that make trouble
for them that must fix it.

"But—well, see
this clean forty-ninth plot
I'm now a-steppin'
was promised to me
by Pastor Olsson as pay
for fixin' the church floor
and cleanin' these grounds,
'n' maybe helpin' him pray.

"It's in this cell where I'm headin'
when my liver spills gravy,
and I'll be proud sure to join up
if your indulgence will have me.
Maybe I'll seem a blight on the boneyard,
and you folks could be takin' it hard.
But just play like I'm yer pertend prisoner,
and you pertend changin' the guard.

"You all know the something or the nothin'
we all wonder up here where it's airy—the details
of dying and of death's sheltering welcomes.
I'd like merry, not scary.

"I guess I'm like any
who coddled a sadness.
I don't blame Ma Nature,
not for Hers nor my madness.
Don't everyone wish for a Heaven
for squaring yer girdle around,
where your passings got lost
and your comings get found,
crossin' to the gain of His Grace
and the loss of all wishes!
But I'll tell you one feeling for true:
the wishin' I have, so I wish it for you."

Back walking the road
and heading for town,
I let my pipe light dance up
over the moon-float near down.
I feel lighter and higher,
as like to God I would holler,
though my night track's still ending
at Hennie's beer parlor.

The sittin' is comfort
with a mug on the table,
and glad I am when Hennie steps out.
He nearways floods liquor
down yer forced open throat,
when he's not too hard a-workin'
at castin' words
in your mouth.

In his moment of absence,
I won't mind tellin' fer once he got tricked.
Hennie goes endless ways talking
about retirin' to that forty-ninth grave
for the dead and the dunked.
Ha! Here Hennie comes now.
Don't let 'm know that he's skunked.
Don't tell 'm he's licked.

A PORTRAIT OF A YOUNG PUD

Boxed and I've never felt so sure,
when I surprise the carpenter at that moment.
But hear the surprise of the tenant!
Be Woo Woo Woo Woo Woo Wufslarf.

When this boy's head emerges from Pud's doghouse,
Pud sputters, *rawr rarrah.*
Not even close quarters and I'm starting to like it.
I'm laughing and talking to Pud to explain this.
Pud has a view.

When his protests were less
of *what the hell are you doing?*
And more to *okay, okay, the show's over,*
I slither from the doghouse,
and hug and rock Pud.
"I didn't swipe none of your stuff, Pud.
No, I didn't filch food from your fridge."

> Maybe when the last atom is dissembled,
> and our genesis finds its tail twixt its legs,
> and those wolf stars stir town lights,
> men, or whoever, then or whenever,
> will write rightly:
> this boy loved this dog.

Don't let trails that you travel
mislead you about dogs,
surmising they go by their nose.
Pud is plying a passel of sensors,
like a satellite.
Pud's panache,
that fizzling sizzle, sniffing the missing,
is fashioned for fun.

Pud fosters foresight for odd optics.
Pud's eyes ponder the toolbox in my hand,
never more completely esteemed,
never seen from more angles,
nor more instantaneously ranked.
Pud's eyes focus, relax, and fondle
the galaxy's gadgets.

For all of that, it is Pud's ears you will envy.
Sieving a masked melody from the habitual hum,
sifting the singer from the cacophonous chorus,
his ears laud a leaf in its leap
and are hoisted at the horrors of hammers.
Rise! And slouch at once,
so that sound may sustain its surprise.

Half collie and shepherd—
see by the white mop hung from his tail,

a rudder wagging our moment. Ears walk.
Snout thrusts toward the middle of me.
His tail seesaws in a bounce that announces
that local time is now, gloriously arrived,
with no apprehension of later. Now arrests now.

Time totes a crescendo!
Wag your buttocks baton.
Will not Nature respond to respect
a kindred orchestral director?
Pud leads beastly bands.
Maestro, grin for a music.
Wave tail at its head.

Has Nature brought a more cautious conductor?
A defiant giant of the minimalist school.
Yet subtle motions emerge in two waves of his wand.
Pud reviles the interpretation of musical scores.
A conductor conducts!
Play the notes, dammit. Don't recreate.

To the robin's allegretto on return to her theme,
to the wild wind's fluid flight through the passage,
to the groan of an oak branch, percussion perfected,
to the shuffling of leaves, began pianissimo,
to the sparrow's cadenza, heard in wing-woven notes,
to the cricket's crisp carol in a theme's syncopation,

allow the next connotation its time,
in the contrapuntal chorus of Pud.

When the next moment leapt, Pud gallops
through a crack in the woods,
as though fleeing this day
and trespassing tomorrow.
I track him with my wits on his prints
till I spy him sniffing the cosmos.
His roam on aroma travels
toward wondrous water,
nearby Union Lake,
where my unbaited fishing rod sits.

With deadwood for pickaxe,
I plow through dark dirt,
surprised to easily find the pink fingers.
Pull seven fat earthworms,
half sliding back in their socket,
pull gently, stretch 'em but keep 'em intact.
Pud provides a positive scentification.
His nose knows them.
And then Pud delivers the sermon for Sunday.

Pud yelps them the facts of their past indirections,
and Pud yawps that to repent
now 'twould be better, for later is waiting.

Those night crawlers face fire
and a sprinkling of brimstone.
Their two ends seek to slink to two exits.
Pud even lambasts me in his preaching,
his sermon for sinners,
when I drop the angleworms
down my shirt pocket and contrive
a cozy cradle for hermaphrodites!

On this dazzling day, our stroll
bestows a bright hike in large light.
At Union Lake, the first worm winces,
impaled on the hook for my line.
A blood drop deals pain from a piercing,
but not mine, for once, this time.
On the end of a ten-foot wood dock,
with water so clear,
the sky reflections emerge muddy
from touching the bottom.
And I cast out my line just to hear
the perky kuh-blop.

Slower than sloths, I draw in the line.
That fat worm coasting so dainty,
I would bite it myself.
A wind whirls over my lake,
blown in from Heaven.

Absolute Light dents the water,
and the farthest green is seen across it.
The Lord lends me this Day—
and some days yet to praise it.
Then two sunfish start approaching
my receding worm,
not a bit in a hurry, just looking.

Again and again, I throw out the line,
so slowly bringing it back.
Again and again, the two sunfish
slither like worms,
a foot behind the worm on the hook.
What a sight we must muster for two sunfish.
Me, gleaming in the sun—
a fierce meteor under the clouds.
Pud, screaming and warning them,
dances by my side.
No need to teach fish,
"Lead me not to temptation,"
when the tempters haven't the brains of the bait.

After the fifth cast,
the two sunfish still follow my hook,
all the while casting sidelong glances
at each other and jesting,
"A nice day for a swim,"

and "Would you get a load of him?"
and "The short one seems smarter,
but the tall one is nicer,"
and "Are they a pair for the suffocating air!
Thank the Almighty they stop at the shore!"

It feels to me like I keep casting out
unanswered questions
and, mercifully, wasn't teased by the nibbles.
I start laughing along with the fish,
thinking this is as happy as I will be in my life.
Futurity affords affirmation.

This once in my life, I ask God
to try painting my portrait.
I'd think of God as an Impressionist, like me.
But God knows the best
about what the scene should reveal
about Pud and the sunfish and me.
I'd probably get taught new and true angling
in God's perfect portrait.
Pud might manifest every dog,
and each dog catches His Day.
God's portrait would broadcast
I finally found out that hour.

After the fishing, Pud and I
lie in the grass by the woods.
We examine our remarkable paws,
and he enjoys this at first.
Then he rocks himself standing,
then off and out running.
Be Woo Woo Woo Woo Woo Wufslarf.
Pud braces his bowed body
to bellow and bounce.
He rummages the remote,
hunts for the hidden,
seeks the unsung, tracks the transcendent.

He looks past the flat, faraway horizon.
Be Woo Woo Woo Woo Woo Wufslarf.
He conceives something out there,
something approaching, something encroaching.
I am silent in the upsurging backdraft
of now's falling and passing.
Pud would've written here:
"More canvas! More oil! More Artists!"
I write here that the Portrait is done painted.

LOCK & KEY

I hold this fish atop the page,
above the screen,
between you and me.
In front of me,

it seems big to you,
while I am small.
I am here
behind the fish.

I left my keys
in my other pants.
I only knew when I arrived
right here, and I have no key.

I chose to go back home,
not knock on your door,
not ask of you.
I will be back.

I braced against the coiling night.
The crowding wind
nudged my nightshirt,
drove drafty dreams through windowsills.

Whisked and whiffed,
a storm respires,
a windpipe rousing
my reel and rod towed by this fish,

in gust and gale,
in watery wind,
the huffing there,
the going somewhere.

Here might a tempest sweep a story,
erase assurance,
blow over history,
and never blow out its own voice.

BATTERY PARK, NYC

The Hudson hatches a noisy thinking river
at Battery Park.
A ceremonial sunset chalks the four lobes
of the baggy, sagging brain of a beast.

The creases, the ridges, the wrinkles, and the crinkles
grow green, like green tarnish on my golden watch.
Whitecaps keep jumping from a river too full.
No other river wanders so watery.

Soft suds lather our Liberty.
Some rivers quietly clap any warning.
Here does Hudson slap at the pier
as a child slaps at the bath.

Ellis Island seemed the farther removed
as I viewed her visage from a coin telescope.
But I returned here at dusk for the fishing.
My Monday hooked a twenty-pound bass,

with a seven-ounce sinker and tuna fish bait.
Between four foreign, green towers
and American whitewater,
on Ellis, I caught her.

RATSKELLER MUNICH

A fool for a frosty fräulein,
I catch her fall in December.
In Munich bright night,
the snowflake tumbles toward me.
She's somewhere now in my stein

of steaming Glühwein.
She's hot spiced wine
moseying the Marienplatz
and the Christmas market,
near nirvana, near the Nativity scene.

The Glockenspiel tattles the times.
Marionettes march when she chimes.
The mechanical midget men must remember
an action taken,
a path forsaken.

My ears and eyes cascade from the clock,
when I alight near a darkness,
one that nests nigh to me.
Then did my clockwork unwind and uncoil
down the great wooden staircase

to Ratskeller.
Stir starry stories of a hive humming,
of manifold multitudinous caverns,
of oak beams and stone columns,
of wrought-iron chandeliers.

Fancy a festive, fond cellar sprawling,
knotted in mystery, a castle crevasse
boasting barrel-lined walls, stained windows,
ornate pillars, vaulted ceilings, with songs
sung in barbed Bavarian consonants.

Rathaus city hall gargoyles,
above ground of this cellar,
wander as wide as their sky.
Here in this fable-flung fantasia,
my gums gambol agape.

The clock's chimes toll a time to taste Weiss beer
and Bavarian duck with red cabbage and dumplings
und spätzle, meine Freunde.
I point at the menu to order,
though it is written in English.

Then the clock chimes, "Weiss Wein,"
for the white wine list is finer.
Practice the parlance betwixt the gargoyles' lips.
Proclaim a parley with a clock's marionettes.
I spot the spell in the cellar. I rise to the Rathaus.

COPENHAGEN IN KØBENHAVN

A comfort, a calm,
in a weightless white sky.
For me, just enough light
to bar worry.

Get me a cool drizzle
to rinse my thought.
My mind opened in entry
and closed on the advent.

What a young household!
All those girls on the bikes!
I shall straddle the bike lane
and rupture in rapture,

and spill into a canal,
a canal bound for the sea.
I will harbor in holey worlds,
and will finally fluidly fit.

I love the statue at Kongens Nytorv,
wherein a horse walks over a man.
Let every conquering jockey, thereupon,
flatten the cocky and talky.

A white cross on red hovers.
Fabrics franchise our fraternities.
Colors claim their place in our planet.
Flagstaffs fly history. Hereafter holds mystery.

At sunset, the pastel row houses
on the Nyhavn canal cast gold,
roosting nearer to never and farther from ne'er.
I know I once knew this. Because I was there.

SEATTLE OPERA & PARADE
(AS TOLD BY ALBERICH IN 1986)

On an aisle seat, I sailed to Seattle.
A dangerous diva prowls
in my head,
and in the Ring Cycle.

Wagner's opera floats a fable arisen
from the riddles of the Rhine River realm,
concerning Man's scuffles with the heavens above,
and our struggles in choosing between power and love.

On that eve, I blundered upon a street cavalcade.
And though Wagner's stage ranks as the greatest,
I, who hated parades,
now was charmed by Seattle's staged latest.

If opera is great music and bad theater,
let parades be the arena
for marching its madness,
the opera of obstruction and asphalt.

One man on a trailer sang a song
I never have heard.
He gestures at us as he sings,
assured that we share our common confusion.

Dim pastel lights, the pink and the green,
conscripted me in an avenue's traveling conspiracy.
Some serious socialites rolled in a rickshaw,
but I don't think they want me to clap.

Here patrolled horses, trampolines, ambulances,
and, after a dragon, came a police paddy wagon.
The band played a leitmotif I know.
"Anchors Aweigh."

I spied a dog's tail below me
as my step bruised his baton.
Tonight, he howled at my blunder.
Tomorrow, I'd howl at blunders-to-be,

when Siegfried's anvil got split
before sword set it asunder.
The curtain got tangled,
the scenery dangled.

In Wagner's opera, the Rhine maidens
brandish blue curves.
Their song simmers, possessing my passion.
They run on the river. I stir at each step.

But tonight, the street parade maiden
sported a crown and a gown,

and she smiled and waved,
then looked straight at me.

This waving girl stopped waving
when I waved.
Her smile sunk
like a marsh headstone.

Wagner's mythical dwarf placed a curse upon love
to gain dominion in depth, to gain Rhine River gold.
I shall renounce love
to recover rule of myself,

to gain love's lasting lapse
and lose love's lusty leverage.
I shall repudiate the marvels of maidens
to find mine in the runes of the Rhine.

BOSTON LONG WHARF

Upon a Boston wharf, a time ago,
the harbor pier posted green pillars,
a row of rotting teeth at low tide.
Stained rings swathed the stakes,
standing in line, fat in the mud,
and carved in the belly.

A wind-whipped newspaper descended,
swept from the shore.
The gazette blew past, willfully,
a debilitated dove.
The public press began flying,
pausing, and waiting.

The front page somersaulted,
launched in three planes,
before settling and sitting
on the harsh harbor water,
on the pliable podium,
on a paradisical pulpit,

in the black cracks of green water,
as watered-down wisdom, the way of all paper.
After a grasp at the sparkles that tickled its skin,
the news sank slowly and straight, as though

lowered by lasso from the grip of my eyes,
down from my seeing, on the plummeting pallet.

This wind is my ocean,
a gassier ward in the world.
Wind whisked the harbor hard to this pier.
The water looked like a river, there by a calm sea.
I am a sailor sought by both boundless realms,
but never sought as a treasure.

A fish leapt from airy spray at the border,
after prey, or as prey,
or spurning a paramour's spawn.
Let me leap to chase the wake of the day,
sprung from the water, cast as a draught,
sought by a down-and-out drought.

FIREFLY

You're as good as me,
but I like me best.
How can I oblige you today?
Truly, I seek to feather my nest.

Fireflies are streaks from a point,
not a point.
I am still able to switch them on and off,
in June, as you know.

I sometimes light a red one
in late July,
but best like to ignite about five
in a June drizzle.

With five, I'll locate the loner.
The four may go lost,
be hot for naught.
But the fifth flickers conviction.

The fifth is the secessionist chemist,
who commits arson on air,
who neglects the plans of God, guns, and girls.
For his singular realm does he care.

HOW WOULD YOU LIKE YOUR EGGS?

In lifting, you'd figure
to find holy honey inside,
not a lugubrious liquor
nor a stone in white hide.

Crack a little and you will
crack a lot.
You cannot partially spill
or pour it somewhat.

Galactic gold in a syrup,
glittering globe in a hollow,
forecasting a chick's chirrup,
or a most perfect first swallow.

I prefer the fright face of the fried
to the bald brow of the boiled.
Leave the lava's yellow aside.
I like crusty edges, butterball oiled.

Never store in the freezer nor leave in the sun.
I care about eggs, their flesh, and their flowing.
Try not to crack her before the bacon is done,
before the rooster renounces his crowing.

Roosters rouse my suspicion.
Only hens snuggle eggs warm.
Mistrust a rooster's volition
to father or foster or feather the farm.

I STOLE FROM ME

A thief snatched the French fries
from my flourishing food stand.
He ran like a rabbit,
but I run faster than vagrants.

I seized him by the rags of his collar.
"Pay up,
or I'll procure payment
from the skin of your hide."

Then he gets all indignant:
"I guess you need a meal more than me.
I want to return these potatoes,
so you won't gadabout hungry."

How dare he deign to gift me my goods!
How dare he stoop to indulge me with favors!
As if he snatched virtue from the void to oppress me,
as if the Lord leapt on his side.

He sought to soar slightly since now I'm so tiny.
I felt my oxygen snuffing. I strived not to crumple.
My face began flushing. My heart held a hammer.
But I fumed in my fury. God raced to erase me.

I searched for an elixir to abolish my shame.
I was angry at God and still irate at the tramp.
I attempted to get even with Him and the thief.
My assets mean nothing. I shall prove it to them.

As grand as a monarch, I issued my edict.
I sought to loom tall but sounded so small.
Too loud, too proud, too unbowed,
I evangelized, "Keep it!"

LAMPSHADE

I didn't need the second look
to know the man,
to glean and trace the path he took.

I once heard a liar say,
"Don't judge a cake by its can,"
when that's the sure way.

One look is expeditious.
A second peek lets them sneak.
And the third glimpse is repetitious.

Why would I grant his guts an appendix,
when I now know each chapter and stanza,
the state of his mortar and his skeletal bricks?

I say give every man a third chance,
but give no man a second.
Find in the third and the first an accordance.

When did we start denying everything we've seen?
My thought is it started with the advent of the lamp,
not the light in a lamp, but its shifty, shady screen.

Lampshades dim and disguise our life lights,
splattering sparkles, the halo in the hearth.
Razored rays get lodged in fragmentary flights.

On a third chance, they commit their last acts,
lifting the veil, launching light from the lantern,
overflowing, glowing with inflexible facts.

HEAVEN AND HARRY

It is written that the Foolishness
of God
is wiser than men.

I've shaken and sifted that thought
today
and spoke to my wife, Mary.

Mary, how could any man be himself
in Heaven,
when his crude thoughts defile him?

How could God fill His household
with snickers
and His wind with near laughs?

Mary said the core of me would park
there.
And my coarse garments would fall away.

I think I may know the man I'd beget
then.
But I wouldn't be Harry.

I once thought we had one up on God.
Here's why.
Only men know what it is like to not be God.

And now Mary says, "He's even got you on that
one.
Christ was a man of dunes and scintillas of Sun."

God was even a lot, lot better at being mortal
than I am.
If I were in charge, I'd sure dodge show-and-tell.

But stubbornly, I fancy a new man sits inside me,
worth saving.
But first, filter the filth from his frame.

I bet after the sieves and the strains,
I'm distilled
into that saint that I've sought.

"I believe it is me!" I will say to modified Mary
in Heaven,
with fond Foolishness,

as the former fool who found faith in the Father,
abandoning
the understanding of Harry.

WHO LEAVES

The deep hollow in a hushed orchestral pit
below me, the maestro, met a calamity.
Fidgety strings and forlorn horns lay listless.
They lay loyal to me, a leader who leaves.

Upon leaving, I left
an audience anxious.
Upon leaving, I abandoned
a symphonic assemblage.

My leaving launched
from my grieving,
following a summons
from a compatriot conductor, outdoors.

One oak tree sought my assistance.
She stooped toward the sidewalk.
She tried to pick up her tumbledown leaves.
She fancied she'd dropped a basket of fruit.

In autumn, I first saw her
with a bushy red skirt,
atop her lost roots,
around her address.

When I prowled in the night
through the lights, for my safety,
I wandered wet layers of leaves,
fall's fronds, rained orange into sheets.

Forsaken, forgotten, the foliage
convened as a curtain, collapsing,
blown into blankets,
sleeping in strata.

I dawdled after the dusk,
along their shepherding handprints.
Each damp leaf pasted orange
to the pavement.

Each palmprint scattered like raindrops
on the trail where I tread,
each clutching the walkway,
each crusting my carpet.

At night, I gathered
the trove from the tree.
And I brandished a maestro's baton,
sweeping the swarm into song.

MISSOURI MANSIONS

My house wrecked.
Now find her abandoned,
aged, a decaying derelict
moored on the muddy floor
of the River Missouri,
where paddle wheels stirred.
Ruins of sunken steamboats
emerge in the drought at low water,
some singing the legends,
a sunken century heard.

From the frail hand of the night,
dropped a trickle of light
on the mansion immersed,
the hogshead and jackstaff,
the bunks by the keel,
by the yawl, by our stateroom.

Come away, hear a way,
slide, and let slip
from the rote,
wrote and rehearsed,
of huffing Mankind.
Far away, find a way,
ride again

the awaiting steamship,
awaiting ahead
and awaiting behind.

Again, to the goings,
with the water-wind blowing
o'er ringbolt and rudder,
o'er sawyer and snag,
o'er fantail and dolly,
o'er hawser and bitts.

Her hull harbors in humus,
in the cracks of her crown.
She took her bow
to the flat bottom,
with keel, boom, and stern.
A steam drum worries this water,
and amid water she plows.
From boiler to smokestack,
there's water to burn.

Aboard, climb aboard,
on my boat's muddy carpet,
in wall-to-wall wet.
Near the surface sod's sanitarium,
find this embalmed deep aquarium.
Find the perishing bell ropes,
past the capstan and kedge.

Steam-sleep in the cradle
of a boat in such rustles,
with water moccasins
cuddling its bones.
As paddleboat Prince,
I forage and chew mussels
with my masseter muscles,
never cleaner than now,
in around-the-clock rinse,
counting fins for no profit,

leaving all numbering off it,
storing crayfish and clams
in the wavering wheelhouse,
and wild celery in the calm calliope.
I will startle the dive of a dabbling duck.
I will pester the prying mind of an otter.

Find a hundred or more mansions
below the Missouri,
always a vacancy
in these paddlewheel inns,
in the flurry of catfish,
in the resident ripples,
no concern for the plumbing,
no wake-up call hassles.

After daylight traverses,
the nightlight begins,
sinking something beloved,
sunk while we're standing above,
wrecked, abandoned, and lost,
embedded in mud.
My sentinels trust me alone.
Tonight, I wade to my room.

MOMENT

I wrote this on contact,
after the ball fell,
but before it could bounce.

I thought this one moment
boxed one beat in the cadence,
the sole one since the past.

It jittered a jolt at the juncture
between serial waves,
at the end of a tempo,

and at a new beginning of me,
the briefest occasion,
before what happens next.

I think I will alter my plans,
just to bother the past,
only to annoy the rest of the day.

Before I poke my head through this gate,
tell me, how much prior art am I required to cart?
I see my chance to leap the length of the pinhole,

provided you stay where you are or move back.
It was your mistake to have waited.
I stopped right about here before forgetting

to let our hereafter alight.
The drummer keeps waving his gavel at me.
I suppose in an instant I'll fall

and fly to a future.
I almost feel it commencing
at the end of a thump.

I only hope you stay home
and don't journey with me,
the way you do, always.

You caught me filling my pockets,
but I'm only taking my things.
Please keep the rest.

I won't need the remainder.
Nearly nearing a segue,
but not presently present,

right now, and wrong then,
I'm conscripted to nibble
each morsel of Time.

MEMORY

On this day, a carpet of leaves
skirt the family trees.
Autumn sunders and weaves
and musters a muddle of memories.

I foretell a parable,
recalled from the second it sailed,
a tale of a parched petiole
and a leaf who leapt to Heaven but failed.

Match a fallen leaf
to the minutia of memory.
Each droplet of diary rains a bit of belief,
drizzling dismembered, yet still tumbling free.

Pair a fallen frond's famous show
with the frailty of well-seasoned thought,
the thoughts squirming my mind, one blunder ago,
thoughts once courted, once coveted, now caught.

Fancy a fallen leaf
as a phantom forgotten, for now,
till then retrieved, in an eternity brief,
as today's passing persuasion, to illustrate how

scholars unravel a mosaic of memory
into each plume of a pliable plan.
First, untangle a petal's pedigree,
then unscramble a man.

I've wondered this week
which memories prove true.
Not timeworn thoughts—no, I seek
inaugural thoughts, when first sprouted as new.

A brain's rain-lathered leaves
may inspire, may nourish, may alter
a bowery of thieves,
or a head in a halter.

Did you see my lost thought?
My name's on that memory.
I adore and deplore its deposit.
Memoirs provoke new antiquity.

NATURE

Consider my rations to Nature.
I exhale each biotic miscue
to refurbish the rubric
of Her forested fabric.
She nibbles my vapors,
my flakes, and my waste.

She's a gobbler,
and, having tasted my flour,
She awaits the gorge of my pastry.
My transfiguration
will chance upon the charry,
but chaste.

She writes my farthermost fate,
the date and the hour.
She displays, as a keepsake,
my souvenir carbon.
She's a collector, an editor,
of my gluttonous glossary.

Will Her chlorophyll glow greener,
Her carotenoids oranger,
now that I'm the bridegroom
of Nature?

She's giddy in foretasting
our forthcoming nuptials.

Never park in the path
betwixt the goddess and her groceries.
Many a corporeal sweetheart
nosed my savory loaf,
knew its gustable gusto,
sniffed its succulent bouquet,

then alas, then aghast, then aggrieved,
bit to the blighted recesses
in the pith of the man. 'Tis for Nature
to uncover Her sweetmeat, Her sweetheart,
in my acrid substratum,
in my despoiled subsoil.

NORMAL

Nature is normal.
Now, people are not.

I, the Past, waggle the begone
and compel you to prove passive.

Let the Former forecast
the puissance of the past.

Let prior precedence
pantomime the first lasting last.

We both know I, the Past,
am never repeated.

Every time, something new,
with unremarkable resemblance to Me.

But I, the pale Past, have crept up to today,
though fear is not even my forte.

I rather prefer to prescribe pianissimo voices,
provided you gather the guts to murmur at all.

I told you to spread my spinning spilled water
until no one finds a drop in the hopper.

I told you to hate your private achievements
and exalt families of failures.

I, the Past, am your master,
and I am who I'll say.

I write my own script
and enforce my own law.

What just happened that's past?
It was your chance to resist.

A DINER'S DUMPSTER

Among the coleslaw and Cobb salad,
in this dumpster's mushy, mashed menu,
I spied a bowl of potatoes,
sauce-slathered chunks in its cargo,
with yet red coats, all the rougher to eat.

Soon enough, would I tell
if these taters saved their savor,
if the white sauce left them firm,
if the potatoes knew a worm,
if the spuds kept the taste of this tuber.

Fresh at the dumpster, as fresh as my rump,
and soon to be gnarled in my chompers, long
before my next dump. After the crowd clears,
I'll kiss all my tots without publicity fears,
when potato, thee, begets potato, me.

One press and roll 'round my ten tattered teeth,
and I knew 'twere a slice of an apple, I eat.
Ain't that the path of this world?
Ain't a plan that ain't curled!
Ain't one heckle nor hector not hurled!

Next time, I'll finagle a menu
from the maître d' of this dump.
Then, I can entreat my entrée.
Even with grub lookin' nice,
here ya still gotta shop twice.

OUT OF DOORS

Fine pine abounds outdoors.
Else, houses would be out of doors.
Nature nurtures my noggin,
but the outdoors dodges my desires
to dump my dilemmas
on her side of the door.

Grandma Nature can't carpet
my walk through her woods
to match the muse in my mind
with the prose of her prickles,
and I pass in her sanctum
more sieved than dissolved.

Though, with frightful delight,
I discern she keeps an eye on it all,
for I spied her surveilling
the dolls of this damp forest,
as a windblown chaperone
to the drifting dandelion seeds.

The underground awaits
for the fall of these skirts.
A fluttering flotilla of fluff
will waft and will hover

for a loiter, a stall,
and a docile descent.

In these north woods,
I devoured scoot berry fruit
from its staircasing stalk
and delicate bells.
I ate these runs-rousing red berries,
and now my fecal effluvium flows

till my squeezed squirts fell
upon righteous bunchberry blossoms,
and upon the malevolent baneberry,
in parallel portions.
Yea, e'en the medicinal wintergreen
gained my crisp blight and bouquet.

And grateful I was for the patch of fat aster,
the blubbery leaves and chubby green hearts,
balled up to mop my mucilaginous mess,
the film on my fracture, the veneer on my vent,
swabbing softly my cleft and conduit,
to erase a rueful mistake concerning a fruit.

If today I wandered wasteful in nature,
recall who is watching.
In each plane between trees,

I see her door as her tempter. I await
all day in these woods for her summons.
You! Enter!

WHISTLE

I am not my face.
I am my whistle.

I would slant my face
another way,
not for vanity,
rather, to annul your sum
that I am a face.

I am the blink of my whistle,
not the whistle you heard,
though I am a fine whistler
and could craft a career
in a cosmopolitan culture.

I am instead the sketch of a whistle,
the nick in the tooth of the whistle,
the thought that the whistle
could tremble or try,
could surprise.

My lamp lost a light bulb.
It had flickered for weeks.
It whistled on, off, and on.
I did not have to replace it.
I just had to tighten its thread.

It had sought *off,* to light its liberty.
Now it is *on,* as bright as before.
I am now likewise unscrewed,
but your wrench could revive me
if you know the number of turns to a whistle,

else, I won't be the same.
Wring me to that forbidden, unfrequented fit
that afforded me harbor,
that rendered me humor,
that warranted my whistle no namesake.

DREAM

I ascended and bobbed through the surface
of slumber, an outgoing guest of a dream.
Upon slipping her last sliding strands,
I fished for the phantasmal fabric of my fable.
I recalled only the texture, the threads of a thrill,
but not the weave of the weeds.

I plunged to plummet back into the pool,
on the hem of awoken,
and thought hard on soft blankets
to force flotsam to find me
and summon the surf to surround me,
awaiting, awaiting awaking.

DYAD

A dyad consists of two parts,
but nothing consists of two parts.
So, we posit the presence of pairs.
A piglet and a grape
deliver a dyad in shape.

I propose one piglet can prance as a dyad.
I grant one grape can dance as a duo.
If the piglet ate the grape,
two pieces still tarry, like sisters,
among the nephews and nieces.

Grapes resemble the piglets.
Aggression erupts in the litter,
then subsides
as dominance gets dispatched
by your submissive behavior.

I'd nudge you aside,
or I'd peck you hard to harness
and hoard my teat ownership,
if we were piglets
before we were grapes.

I can't leave my home
without brawling in dyads,
even though I would avoid you,
if I could avoid winning and losing
at my feeding priority.

Wine lovers weigh first the color
to indicate grape quality and age.
Ruddy blue or brick red,
someplace, grace a grape vintage,
a dyad from duplicitous vantage.

On another side of the dyad,
my wine rates as subordinate,
and renders irreverence in its inferior rank,
with acerbic astringent aroma,
seeped from the skin and the seeds.

But the best of the color will bloom.
Slow, slow, do the dyads evolve.
Slowly, wine pigments polymerize.
Slowly, sediments precipitate.
Slowly, lees bleed, shedding dyads of dregs.

EATING ICE

Through dark windows of my speeding train,
a gargantuan car lot in yard lights kept throbbing,
whisking rearward waves in a hurry,
severing the chain links of cars.

We love people
whom we've aided,
more than we
love people who aid us.

Reading her newspaper,
over her shoulder,
in the train café car,
made the news interesting.

I chewed upon words.
I'm eating ice
until its fiber defrosts,
until a clinging truth brushes a tooth.

But I'm eating ice, and my rectitude slips
on the words dripping out, melted
in my flaming brain, chipped by the crossing
from my eyes to my lips.

ALIVE NOW & THEN

I entered alive,
this bright moment of life,
just now,
alighting alive,

though I lacked longings to love it enough,
and now the moment's completed.
Each moment conjures a crisis in life.
Only memoirs and maps seize esteem.

I have admired my diary
and diagram.
I've enjoyed what I seem
and no less what I sent,

though this picturesque moment
feathered a featureless portrait.
A big band of bells burbled somewhere,
across then and between now.

I BELIEVE

The sea flows flat
despite each dithering dimple,
bouncing up, sliding down,
half believing its pulse.

I live in a nation
redacting religion, but rendering
a reclusive reverence
for its mysterious ripples.

Keeping quite busy,
I've learned which buttons to push,
and I harbor high status
and self-worth.

Am I above or below
the circumference?
I believe the next graph
will come as a comfort.

Hover habitually smug, if you must,
and taunt a church steeple.
But each breath is drawn or driven
as a gratuity, a grandiose grace given.

I spy a sky as blissfully blue as the sea.
I sit on a bicycle, and my legs
will impel it, compel it,
I believe.

MY BOY

Emergent again,
my father retells the story
of the day I was born.
The particulars and paragraphs vary.

Sometimes, he'd remember his pride,
when the nurse narrated the news,
regarding the hospital hysterics.
His farm chores were paused and postponed.

But the story will touch on its climax
when he held me
and vouched, veritably,
"That's my boy."

I loved the lad in this legend,
though I'd never confessed
he'd invented my glory.
I loved the boy in our story.

When he hoisted me up,
he'd annulled the ways
of the world and rescinded
the malfeasance of boys.

He neglected to forecast
a single caper I'd consummate.
He wouldn't acknowledge
that the world could come into me.

He held a baby
who is holy,
who defies the world
and its girdle.

I still foster flickers of fancy,
when I'm the way that he tells it.
I think of that infant, my dad's trustworthy toy.
That's my boy.

SAN FRANCISCO UMBRELLA MAN

On Market and Fourth,
What is the worth
of this here umbrella
I could sell ya?

I reckoned 'twere merely
a rare drizzle,
and so brooked nary a barter,
but soon it rained harder.

Why'd I shun the plan
of the San Francisco umbrella man?
Maybe my forecasting floundered,
or maybe my desires conspired.

Maybe I wished for a five o'clock wetting.
My drenched dorsal dome was fooled into forgetting
my heart's ventral, venerable plan,
to end juvenile jollies and behave like a man.

It couldn't stop raining.
I'm as soaked as a saint.
But I ain't complaining.
My corporeality's draining its paint.

I spy, in the torrent, young faces
approaching, encroaching.
I bob in a bay younger than yonder,
more buoyant than my boyhood oasis.

Wet birds peck round and round
my slippery sidewalk,
for a savory worm, waiting their turn,
in a feast fit for a flock.

Now we all wear black coats,
a shadowy shade,
wet, wayward wardrobes,
in an arcane cavalcade.

We brandish bathed brains
in the raiment of rain, vouching
our vows to avoid, to evade,
our fated fuming and fade.

BAY AQUARIUM

Posted placards say we're bad, wall wisdom
in the aquarium hatchway. Blather!
Am I the one drinking the Bay?
Always our fault and not yours,
but you're the one dredging
the channel for tankers,
which need twenty feet or mud stuck.
The Bay metamorphosed over millennia.
Well, that's my age, too, if by eon or epoch,
sans senior discount in price of admission.

Saw a circle of silver,
silver anchovies,
in a big cylinder tank.
I'd, too, circle this silo in silence,
no righteous ranting from me.
The swarm is on time
and always swims clockwise,
seen here from above them,
though they'd orbit counter the clock,
beheld from below.

Do I bandy big eyes and a big open mouth?
Or am I the small fry you fancied?
Submerged societies sanction

the big to swim with the big,
and the small with the small,
and apart from us all.
Now, off to the elevators,
and on to the petting tanks.
I might snuggle a skate or cuddle a ray,
if I dare to thrust my hand in the sand.

"Just leave me alone," so says a big stinging stinker.
But amongst underage skates and raw rookie rays,
you'll always find an eager beaver,
bobbing her head to the top, wishing to pet me.
What beauty blossoms in the big bass a-swimming!
Fish are all failures. They can't shove water away.
I felt your force, as though myself in your muscle.
But I hover in harbors of the hydrogen bond.
I am the space you displaced.
Now I recoil, flowing forth, rolling back.

PIER 2

By a city of broken paths
and curled course,
I walked till walkways spray sprinkles.

A scoop of the bay sopped my eye sockets.
And my fancy flew, floating o'er the pier,
caroming off whitecaps on wind-woken water.

As I bounced to the beat of the boats,
their prancing masts thrust
accusing fingers toward the sky,

where they probably suppose I reside.
Still, I could nap 'neath the bay bridge
that crouches to cradle a tramp,

buoyed atop this blithe blanket,
with a sea breeze bubbling the broth,
blown up, rocking, and pocking its plane.

The sky borrowed blue to the beckoning bay,
which bandied blue, too, brushing the far shore.
The white waves stopped stirring, way over there,

where a gray bridge greets a green island
at an aimless angle, not north, nor east.
And so, I suspended my sense of dimension,

and I thought I slept on the sea
till the wharf's sea lions passed,
returning to extinguish their unlighted lamp.

ROGER

I sprang upon writing,
writing in earnest,
with passion, with ardor,
when my pen suffered a seizure,
and complied with coercion.
Roger dragged an inky diagonal
across my profound page.

My horror!
But Roger was laughing.
And I laughed with Roger.
I'd thank Roger the better
for his effacing revisions if he
supplied the help that I'm needing.
Let Roger's redactions

edit all the books
that we're reading,
before revoking my writing.
Resolutely, I write a line
and cross swords with my Roger.
Boys can laugh better than men
if men can remember.

Boys can laugh better than femmes,
for they laugh over men.
I laughed with my dearest childhood friend,
Roger.
Did you know Roger was merry?
A roistering nonchalant-ic,
an impetuous skeptic,

a rollicking frolic-le,
a cavalier, care-canceling sprite.
Though our stories strayed from elation,
Roger's raillery rendered jests of our jams,
and we blathered our books in burlesque.
Before college, we parted,
for I am a bookworm,

and Roger teaches guitar.
Try Mozart to think of the meter of Roger.
The tiniest task launches a laugh
for the strings. But call me, then,
a composite of composers
from any andante, the sad satisfaction.
Though lately, I've been getting the Rogers

while writing, and it's beginning
to vex me, fearing this man will yet
steal from my gloom

and subvert my vocation.
If, in the surprising event, there is yet
one poet in want of a foil,
take Roger.

A PEPPER'S HEAT

Capsaicin combusts a pepper's panache,
the flamboyance that festers
in her swagger and dash.
The sap spills to hasten its harsh inspiration,
a sweltering censure, a scalding sensation,
trapped in its lacings, staining the tongue
in torrid, tart tracings, in the unlighted flash.

Weigh heat by its absence.
Dilute heat till it turns tame
to you, feeling agreeable heat,
seeking tolerable burns.
A pepper's heat flickers,
filled by the soil,
or fell from the stars.

Be a wolf's eyes.
Be twice forward,
but a little apart,
to see the depth
of the inferno,
to see the limits
of sting.

And be the eyes of a mouse.
Be aware of the sideways.
Be away from both places.
Be in its bosom, the middlemost deep.
Risk ruin till your torch tingles,
till your blood blazes,
till your flesh flames.

FIRST QUESTION

I nurture my notions.
Why rerun, recount, replay, and repeat?
I've tendered my torments, ten times a trillion.
Never rob a bodega wherein you wouldn't eat.

Never heist a plug nickel
from a corner hole-in-the-wall,
peddling grungy grub in its groceries.
Foul food's your fair warning of a brawl.

I cannot walk past that window
without foreboding deplorable chow,
without a swallow of swill in gestation,
without a rip of arising rank abomination.

Those muffled voices venting the entry
reek as a replicate of its flavorless flotsam,
as though sung to this dunghill by a sentry,
an ode to villainous vittles and odious offal.

Mr. Quiz, you told me you toted two questions.
Of my two answers, you've flouted my first.
Hoist from the holster the point of your pistol.
Take a quick whiz, though the restroom is the worst.

RUNNING THROUGH WINTER

I ran
when the flare of January
consumed the last candles.

My run
from my work to the bus
pushed over the cold,

shoved back the air
seeking to strike me,
the runner.

My footfalls,
the hammer,
the pavement,

the bus,
all fought against air
that harried our harbor.

The girl ahead startled,
for I ran right on past her,
she, who was casual

and content in a coat,
arousing my shame as I ran
from an urban wilderness winter.

And I ran,
to consent to the crux of the cold,
to run from my shame,

to run
from the man and the moment,
to elude this man who is running.

SHEPHERD

I trust the shepherd,
not the sheep.
I defend the dainty,

as the deputy shepherd.
My flock convenes
to adjourn.

I direct my flock
to diminish in
ones.

Join up to quit,
in my freelance flock
of the forthright.

Lambs and ladies,
act as ones,
not as one.

SKUNK

Pooches prefer showers, not tubs.
By porchlight, my dog,
who revels in his rough ranking
and high rectitude,
sprang into a Socratic debate
with a scholarly skunk.

Menaced by premise,
Pooch pummeled skunk's thesis
to pieces, unholy but holey,
just as Swiss cheese is.
With some lasting thoughts
of the quarreler's quotations,

the skunk was extinguished.
My dog was distinguished
at a delicate distance.
For some time,
he remained suspicious
of the mottled who hop.

Pooch never read him his rights,
though at heart, skunks are good,
just misunderstood.
I preached to Pooch the precepts
of relativism,
and he's still smelling my counsel.

ONE PICTURE

Let's let each person's profile persist
in one photograph, only,

all of us truncated
and trimmed to one mugshot,

in one photo that forecasts our crime,
or in one portrait of us, doing time.

You and I would roost unraveled,
untangled, in a singular snapshot.

Dump the shoebox.
Ditch the camera.

Heave the hundreds
of pictures.

Recording is too easy
for the prodigal thumb.

The hot icons
shrivel to still life.

The facsimile slumps
in a quiescent card.

I found the one photo
I will keep—

the baby held by the mother,
who vortexed a volcanic smile,

because she hoisted such happiness,
with no payment or plan.

First, try to tally ten
memories that matter,

not memories assigned,
nor bound to a photo.

Do as I do,
enlighten your library.

You only tabbed ten.
Which one will you choose?

FIRST GENETICS

Not as beads on a necklace,
genes engender
beads of biddable bubbles.

Label each link in your chain,
or mine, for most seem the same,
but drastically differ, my proof—the brain.

Genes gesture as knowable,
paintable, and picturesque
as peas in the pod.

Men and monkeys merge,
sprouting so nearly the same
billion grains.

Yet one single grain grants
the change, launches
a life or a death of a man.

Differences crown all cognition.
Similarity shoes the foot
of our folly.

But tyrants and teachers
ordain my assignment.
I'm trained.

Repeat after me:
not as bubbles,
but as beads on a necklace.

GYM

I was born into the gym
of hard sprung muscles,
of farmers who wrestled
a planet and won.

From their pain and their blood,
from labor's legacy,
you're granted the gift to fake labor,
to mount an affectation of work

in the gym.
Your share of the world's work
zips the zero in n0thing.
Farmers battered and broke their bodies

to feed us.
Their pectorals and triceps
flashed as trifles, as feathers, to them.
Now I tour with the theatrical troupes,

in the pantomime gym,
where sinew purveys lipstick,
where muscle bestows costume,
and the plume portrays its panache.

JACK & JILL: INNOCENT CIVILIANS

Conscription serves better
at condoning
than at condoling.
Jack didn't wish to wage war,
but he died.
Jack was an innocent civilian,
more than I.

Everyone hates the neighbors,
the nations, the world.
But everyone likes profligate precincts
more than the privation of prison.
So, I do not refuse to pay taxes.
I'm not an innocent civilian.
I deserve to be strangled on stage.

Jill paints her self-portrait
to polish
her place in the pigsty.
She feels so bad
about our badness.
She diddles the dictionary
and hoses the historical record,

until Jill jerry-rigs
a lustrous Jill.
Jill sails supremely above us,
one of those not-in-my-name imbeciles.
Solely for my incapability
of inculpability,
I would preserve the innocent girl.

NOBLE

Perchance this year,
the call of the Nobel committee

will kindle no cheer
in our greatest thinkers.

Mr. Nobel phones the notables:
"Sonny, you won a prize."

Sonny snickers and sneers.
"Prizes are for children."

And Sonny, a noble man, continues his career.
Mr. Nobel grows desperate for takers,

and parcels prizes for persuasion,
the namesake of fake makers.

BUS

In half earth at night,
birds bolt from fraternity
with freedom from flight,
from flurry and hurry.

In half earth at night,
birds gather insight
on the symptoms of selfhood.
In half earth at night,

I sit in a bus.
An old man stands
and bestows braised Hades
upon the bus driver

because the schedule was changed.
I ponder the birth of time.
I ponder the end of time.
The old man maligns and molests

our mellow bus driver,
who stares straight ahead,
who laments his license for listening,
and will not take flight in the night.

CADAVER TEACHER

We were destined to meet.
We're meat.
But only I clutch the cleaver.

In medical school, the dead
tailor a tool. Indeed, as a rule,
only the dead rank as cool.

I construe in my cadaver a map,
the slow creep of soap bubbles
in a pan of red water.

I discern self's singularity there,
the precarious chance.
He was born before bypass.

Squeeze the gravel from gallbladders.
Swish the taste on your tongue,
off your finger for fun.

Find the fugitive fervor
of nameless nerve networks,
as white as a wedding dress.

Metabolism moves fantastically fast,
like the legs of a lawyer,
like the lapse of a clock,

flowing faster than sneezing,
or chewing a bean,
or seeing the unseen,

till it bursts like a bubble,
till it tarries in tatters,
torn from the turbulence,

seen in a lab script.
Truth prowls prompt, punctual,
a petulant pig,

while lies linger, as layabouts,
insistent, convinced,
a mystery for history.

I'm dissecting, disentangling, divining,
in my mind's mists, where I, myself,
might moor in my cadaver's imagination.

My cadaver and I sing
from the same song sheet,
but his ledger lines transcend the treble clef.

We've arisen as ripples from a plummeting pebble
plopped in the pond, but his wave fled ahead
while my ridge rolls in arrears.

I map life from the school of the dead.
From the legends of the lifeless,
I learn a loss of my leverage.

ELECTRIC FENCE

I recount my electrons drifting down,
flooding my body, fogging my mind.
I grew as galvanized as a ghost
and as frozen as welds in a toolbox.

Our farm's electric fence bestowed beauty,
shining lines, zinc-frosted wire,
a bovine border known by a herd,
and beheld by a boy.

On this noon in the fleet flow of summer,
my intuition broached barriers,
borders, bulwarks, and boundaries,
and I grasped the wire in both hands.

Biting shackles bound me.
My hands refused to let go,
though sirens in my attic bellowed.
I roiled rigid in hundreds of volts.

Then rocking in my father's lap,
I ingested the story.
He saw from his tractor
me standing, spike upright.

He guessed correctly what happened
and ran to the fence,
and ran through the fence,
releasing its prisoner.

Throughout life, I got bullied by borders.
I've kicked the corral.
I've rattled the ramparts
and even fondled a fence.

Now my rust renders a corroded conductor
for my galvanized guard rail,
in my placated paddock,
in my pasture stockade.

If by penchant, practice, or pageant,
I should again grab the wire
and can't shatter the shackles
of its voltaic vacuum,

prithee, sir, burst through the barricade,
forgiving my folly, like a fear-flouting father.
Treasure the tingle, the trickle of time.
Plow past the present. Flee from the current.

PAUL'S RUMOR

He wouldn't attend his own funeral.
He was Paul,
stubborn-streaked Finn, stoic and steeled.
Try pulling one stalk from his field.
Try it, that's all.

Paul plopped correct change on the counter.
Real men work for a wage, not kowtow for tips.
Ain't no one tipped Paul for driving his tractors.
No rich hogs or old hens were Paul's benefactors,
when Paul shoveled his cattle's gold chips.

Paul moved at an angle set from the dance
with his ornery horse.
The force of his fist dished a skeleton ripper,
deliverin' more stars than Orion's Big Dipper.
Paul never hauled no private remorse.

Door knockers came to collect for the poor
in the jungle. Paul stared them to bits.
"I take a day for my neighbor
when he earns my good labor."
The knocking desists.

Paul would revile a rooster, rousing his rancor
at the dumb duck's dawdle at dawn.
In Paul's chores, the sun seemed a slow helper.
Its slack crack began Paul's work in sun's cellar
as the sun meandered before befriending the lawn.

Find the same empty chair
at the rifleman's meeting,
no joiner, not Paul.
Paul would hunt small, or not at all.
Hunting in hordes borders on cheating.

And Paul ain't cozy with community concerts.
Paul relished music alone, sung by his creek,
not sung by stacks of cheap creaking bleachers,
not sung by squadrons of squat squealing teachers,
nor by your daughter's clarion clarinet squeak.

A blue-fisted, self-governing son of a Finn,
he'd return your dropped penny.
Paul's a man, not the mush men become
when there are more men than one.
But he'd rage as an enemy, if he ever had any.

After the rumor, they hauled Paul to a hospice
to die. Then I hooked a fish from Paul's river,
and I pilfered Paul's famous fish fry.

But the river reflections marked me as a spy,
portrayed me beside Paul, the maker, the giver.

I said to Paul's twin, "I had heard
of your funeral." Paul answered, mad,
like I'd launched an attack.
"Sir, you'll take that back,
or, lad, you'll be sorry and sad."

I have long determined
to honor his wish.
I did take him back.
I never plundered his shack,
though I kept the fish.

LASTING DAYS

She cares for the elders, the weak and diminished,
the invisible wellspring, the planet's pedigree.
She watches them caressing death's docking chill.
The sweater will shiver; the slipper will kick.

Perfunctorily, we posture, prolonging their lives,
though many in dotage half wish they would die.
No words will uplift them,
the helpless, the homeless, the hostage.

She advances his spoon
and empties his bedpan.
The fragrance of bloody feces festers,
thrillingly extreme.

Their loss of dignity inspires her
to serve with dignity.
She grew determined to obstruct and annoy
the foul powers that pounce to destroy.

A twirling tower of lost leaves
outside the window
captivates her, and she fancies
she's mistakenly alive.

The legislators of love are her scourge.
Hear them clucking the cant of compassion.
They fondle feelings to comfort themselves.
They cannot commit to this grandiose grind.

She dispatches duty, but she discovers love.
Love perseveres.
Love transcends emotion.
Love slumps but can't topple.

Love sacrifices until love's service elapses.
Her beloved in beds
continue the conflict,
beyond the crust of our compassion.

NEW MARKET POND, NEW JERSEY

I drove my car to auto mechanics
on New Market Road and marched
home, forecasting my mending,
relishing repair, a revival of rigor,
a flowering of fitness,
feeling staid status soon restored.

I strolled down a cracked sidewalk.
Grass greened all the cracks
in the cement, snapped into plates,
at serrated, aimless, odd angles.
But the fractured slabs
looked benign, watchful,

stalwart, and historic.
This path refused to relinquish its past.
Three women slowly slunk from a church.
There's a funeral, not mine to mind.
I trudged across train tracks.
Rail rust leached into wood ties.

These forsaken tracks felt fallow, felt hollow,
felt to me the void of a vacancy,
laid lost in the before and hereafter.
I sought a traveling train for healing my feeling.

Beneath a bridge, a brook descended a dam,
an unwilful tipper, paddling to New Market Pond.

The pond parked there too quiet.
Fragments of flowers
slumped on the surface,
flagging the flow of the stream.
A submerged rock
broke the pond roof,

attempting to hold back the moment.
Eddies began spinning the clock,
counter to clockwise,
while geese floated like flotsam,
arresting the motion of time.
The whole neighborhood knows it.

Time tarries to breathe,
not brake, not slacken, not stall,
until parceling its passengers
to go ashore, detrain,
desist, duly depart.
In this precinct of Piscataway,

we progress to the proximity
of its periphery.
We abut the border of blank.

We approach a termination of time.
First comes this pause
in the pulse of its cadence.

THE SERVANT

The servant stole eleven scoops
of parfait upon a piece of cake.
She pilfered a spoonful of caviar
and snitched a snifter filled with wine,
to raid the rich, to lap milady's luck,
and not technically to take,
not consciously to plunder,
though one swallow led to nine.

Alas, every morsel moldered.
Dollops drooped upon her tongue.
The sweet cake faked delish,
and the vintage vented vile.
Forecasting famous flavors,
the yearning of the young,
she dangled disappointment
past the threshold of denial.

How oft better grub and grog
she'd relished, even yesterday.
Opulence pledged rapture,
not the swindle of this swill.
Past a drawbridge of a kingdom,
she found the colors gray.
A mischief maker's magic
emerged to fabricate the thrill.

The servant spied milady's purse
perching posh upon a chair.
The squeak it shrieked when opened
seemed the snap of snatched hellfire.
The servant wept. She descried
the depth of this palatial otherwhere
and returned the purse to smolder
in milady's doomed desire.

RICHARD THE APPRAISER

Mom marshaled two marauders, two midgets,
lit the launchings and rolled out the revelers.
Grand garments festooned my womb
as my wobbly wardrobe, secondhand apparel,
pristinely preserved by the previous patron,

my brother Richard, a chivalrous citizen.
Whether in a blastula laguna or vitalized village,
he proved proficient at performing everything
properly. To garner goodwill, he always begat
the befitting, benevolent, best thing to do.

Likely, I left that inaugural roost in a mess, strewn
with rumpling wreckage from my rampant revelries.
No one ever rented that penthouse again. Alas,
my residence roused a reproof of the neighborhood.
Richard married an insightful, enlightened lady,

and, with her, spawned two spectacular girls.
The sisters blossomed like the blush
of a blessing, guarded by gardeners,
guardians who vanquished the weeds.
I've wondered how parents learn to liaise

with lassies and lads. What celestial sightline
suffuses savvy in our moms and our dads?
Bachelors mangle each answer
bequeathed to a child. How do our folks
master the transmogrification of riled to smiled?

Richard traveled northwestern Minnesota
as an appraiser of farms, homes, and land.
His livelihood prospered in countryside jaunts,
and he knew the laughter and legends
of these pastoral haunts, just as he knew

the hallowed hallmarks
of his unsullied small town.
Community club champion,
church council advisor, he promoted
the former and practiced the latter.

You see, big-city boys learn how to blather.
Small-town boys learn how to matter.
If Richard served on every town board
in the land, he'd conjure a climate
of trenchant tranquility for mending

the maelstrom of meddlesome imbecility.
And he'd render righteous rescue
from any mischief the meddlers had planned,

much like the riotous rescues arisen
from the town's Ambulance Squad,

when Richard's posse postponed
a few fellows' appointments with God.
Most everyone here hunts and goes fishing,
royally ranked in the heartland. Hereabouts,
freedom once won stays snug, sacrosanct.

I fancy the great Appraiser
grew joyous, upstairs,
when Richard entered His flocks,
for He hoists a hefty report card,
and Richard's checked every box.

Maybe then an angel inquired,
"Hadn't this exemplar a brother?"
"Ahhh, yes … so he did,"
mutters his mate.
"He was the other."

MAID IN LARCHMONT, NEW YORK

The small steps are mine behind mom's big wheels.
I roll her, she, swaddled in a wooly sweater,
in August. Time: 2:00 PM. Timed: 95 years.
She looks ready for launch into the park—
see her lifting her heels to tour Minnesota.

Golden moss bastes the trees, spots the walkway,
to festoon my happy moments,
enlisted as the motor for Her Majesty's chair,
the mother's son long absent, absent,
now flagrantly there.

Other hands guide her bathroom activity.
I hear her informing the certified nursing assistant,
in a loud whisper,
"That's my son—he's got lots of money."
"Mmm—that's good," says she.

She'd toiled as a farmer's daughter and a farm wife.
I have faith my mother rocked me to sleep
in the manner, I beheld later, she rocked herself
to vivacious visions,
part humming, part singing

the hymns of our church,
so softly and tenderly
rocking on our secret journey
to somewhere
she knew.

I keep postponing my pivotal point
about the reference letter
from the lady in Larchmont, which I found
while jettisoning the junk in her old home,
after her trek to the near-noiseless nursing home.

I purged and expunged closets,
boxes, baskets, and bags.
Sanity says it's all garbage,
but I sought adventure in script
and found out, fantastically,

my mother, then a youth, labored
as a maid in Larchmont, New York.
At least her employer thought so,
and the testimonial tattles the topic
in this letter of reference:

"N— R— has been in my employ six months.
I have found her to be willing, honest, a good worker,
having kept my home very neat and clean.

She cooks well and is an excellent baker.
Also, she washes and irons very nicely.

"I can gladly recommend her to anyone
seeking the services of a good servant.
Mrs. E— J—, Such and Such Street,
Larchmont, New York,
May 1, 1940."

I'd neglected to check my mother's references,
before I launched into life, an egg in her basket.
Indeed, my mother never shared her CV with me,
though I found the lady in Larchmont
posted it, salient and succinct, in retrospect.

But I just couldn't yet see it as real.
Before breakfast, my mother would drain
the teats of eight Holstein cows, returning
with the aroma of manure on her barn clothes
and flaunting the flakes of their feed.

Can it truly be there is a lady in Larchmont,
and she and I shared the same servant?
My questions to Mom on this improbable chapter
brought her brief, almost bored, memories
of grievous grandeur in the late Great Depression.

Her older sisters had strayed first from Minnesota
for maid jobs amongst New York's majestic rich.
Her sisters found a short-term position for her,
and she traveled a train to the east for a season.
She worked for the widow of a liquor importer.

Bottles and barrels beamed in the basement.
"Mrs. E.J. always asked for my taste.
I didn't want to, but I did taste a little."
An outlandish adventure dished up
for the girl from the farm.

Mom dispatched her duties as *my* steadfast servant,
just as well, feigning her fealty to me.
She professed prudence, even evinced a vexation
about venturing beyond the gates
of our secluded farmland, the shepherded shore.

Am I to believe her dubious discourse,
avowing she would walk all alone
through dark woods to the train station
in Larchmont,
for a journey to menacing Manhattan?

She recalled the World's Fair that year,
but it had too much machinery.
She remembered instead the ice cream

and Radio City Music Hall,
sprung outward in a city that shot upward.

While she toiled as *my* maid,
she discouraged adventure beyond acres
of pastoral horizons and secret ravines.
But can it be there is a lady in Larchmont,
and she and I secured the same laundress and cook?

Of course, you know my fancy in this:
one day, I shall knock on that door in Larchmont,
asking the lady herself (and not her granddaughter)
about that servant she recommended,
for I, indeed, found her service as advertised.

I'll say, "Yet tell me, please—"
And then she will say back to me
the same words,
simultaneously:
Who was she?

Find still a peek of amusement
on the nodding gray head of my mother.
The singular soul's slumbering accomplice,
its treasure, its commodity,
is the secret.

Who was the lady in Larchmont?
Who was the son's servant?
Who was she?
Then tell—*who are you?*
Only you will ever know.

THE KITTY & THE FLY

Stacks of baled hay rose
at our cattle farm, erected
twenty feet high and wide.
The bales set stones
in the castle walls,
a ladder to gables and spires,
as I prowled atop my fortress,

not as the king.
My father saw me and finished my fun,
when he showed me the fear.
I suddenly saw the fear clearly,
as though I'd clutched its cold cables,
dreading death.
But I felt fearless to forage
in the fortress dungeon,

where fantastically in a crack between hay bales,
three kittens roosted as moistly warm bundles.
Their charm commands: *pick me up, pick me up.*
Then they see the fear, clearly, and fight.

My father was there then
to hear their *pick me up.*
He picked one up, and his hand

was ripped in the rumpus.
Claws and gnaws, then
his blood blushed from his hand.
I saw injustice.

That moment, my merciful father
said something changing my outlook,
not in full at that moment,
but later, when I mused on the memory.

He said: *They don't know any better.*

I reckon our enshrining love of cats
renders a doomed courtship,
an irremediable rehearsal.
And our reverent love of fathers
launches an ungovernable journey
from an impracticable theater.

On one visit, twenty years later,
to my beloved father and exemplar,
I saw him, as usual, recline
in that stuffed sloping chair,
and I spied the flight of a silent fly,
a silent small fry.
My father reported bites in the night.

Driven by my bitter memories of bug bites,
I swore this bug-thug would atone
for every blood spoiler as I stalked him,
avouching vehement desire for his death,
not breathing hard lest he hear.

I'd not procured the best tool for the job
and stormed stupidly with newspaper clubs.
I cunningly trapped him in the bathroom.
However, then the fly seemed to vanish.

I know that you're here,
and I won't open the door
until I get you.
So, I batted the light fixtures,
and I banged on the walls
and scanned the ceiling
until I nearly gave in.

Then arrived the revelation
of his preternatural stealth.
He had alighted on the one
black surface in the room,
a wastebasket
that nearly mimicked his pigment.
I pretended to not see him.

I rolled up a white towel
and lashed at the wastebasket.
The fly lay stunned on his back.
Satisfied was I
as I squished him in tissue,
buzzing, almost awaking.

On the topic of flies, their kin,
and itching infections,
I spoke to my father later that day,
supposing
we share a passion for fly murder,
whether by chemical can or by hand.

That moment, my merciful father
said something changing my outlook,
not in full at that moment,
but later, when I mused on the memory.

He said: *They've got to eat something too.*

As the years pass and I travel
the path of my father,
we've converged in faith,
in fortune, in habits, in loves,
but not in our infatuations.

The measure of mercy differs
among denizens, when deputized.
A kitty commences a cat,
while execrable flies and their attorneys
connive the next concatenation of man,

singing *pick me up, pick me up,*
and from shadows approach for our blood.
Will you, yourself, pet them or swat them?
Each fellow fixes the fuse of forgiveness.

ANGELA
& THE HOTEL DEL CORONADO

Crowned in Coronado, crafted by carpentry,
The Hotel Del soars supreme from the sea.
Crisp colors convulse on a colossal coast castle.
What painter or pixie posted these hues—
Red riot on turrets, wanton white upon walls,
Godly green upon palms?

What deity dabbed each dot from her brush,
To kindle the canvas in flamboyant flames,
To hoist holy the whole?
Truly, a demigod dwells in Del's dragon tree,
In the grandiose green of her skeleton skin,
In her verdant vined vertebrae.

Howling red hearts menace this mansion,
Wreathing the rooftops,
Festooning the façade,
Adorning the domes,
Of the mysterious manor
At the doorway of the inscrutable sea,

At the brink of the briny,
At the ravishing rims of desolate deep,
At the bewitching border of blue.

Ho, which queen's quarters are quicker?
Which queen conjures the best quest
In our journey to the deliverance of death?

'Tis true, the sea's crypts tumble mystery,
But Del's dwellings harbor history.
Hear your footsteps creaking on stairs.
Beware. Beware of ghosts grasping.
Find your floor squeaking. Fancy your bunkmates.
Heed her heart beating, beating,

Beating, beating her blood
Through torrential turrets above,
Refilling her resplendent red roof.
The dragon tree totes a sack of glistening gold,
A shower of flour, a chowder of powder,
To sprinkle the sand, to sparkle this strand,

To alight white on the shore.
Sun blazes. Del raises a clement, cool milieu
As the sea breezes search for her guests.
Perhaps I was the guest whom Del then regarded,
The guest whom Del ranked miles above
Her capricious companions, her casual cronies.

For I was a man maniacally in love
With Angela.

But possibly Del mistook me for you.
Maybe I arrived unnoted, unsung,
Announced as another. Who would she anticipate
At the porch of the ocean, at the Pacific gate,

At the House of Del,
On this celestial surf-sodden eve
When nightlights sloshed in the sea?
I pronounced *Angela*,
My breath of love fleeing the night,
Soaring over the surf, never to alight

On Coronado sands.
I puffed the appellation,
Angela.
And the House of Del choired as a cathedral,
Gold as a volt,
Till palm fronds atop their towering staffs

Wiped the window of this blackened blue sky
Of December to expose one worshipped star
And disclose one dearest girl,
Serenading my soul.
The surf rumbled
Its slumberous rush of immersion

And reversal. The surf sought to guide
A man in love, as I was, as I am,
To make leave of this longing, as she can.
Passion prowls betwixt the Del and the sea,
Where the corporeal can consort with an angel
And caress the cool tears of this clandestine sky.

Tread the sands dividing the deep and the Del.
Here do the allures for the lovestruck prevail,
A paradisical precinct for the smitten, the bitten,
For the blokes from the bright castle,
For the bewitched and besotted—enraptured
And ravished in this rhapsodic realm.

Somewhere circling the surf,
Angela tendered her trance,
The whisper of one word,
To forecast the flash
Of my flinch at her entrance:
Angel. Angel. Angela.

Del's dragon tree brayed from bedchambers,
A glow at my back, a tug on my belt.
Crossing white sands, my footfalls sunk in the soil.
Then by ear did I know, I stood at the border of go.
Under ministry of the moon, in the nebulous night,
Surf glided over the grains of the shore,

Secretly seeking, softly sliding away
Without prey,
In ponderous pondering pulses,
In puffs of persuasion,
Where a sea whispers and flatters
To snare me

At earth's boundary.
In the stealth of the starlight
At the brink of bright Del,
I kept my eye on the tongue of the surf,
The last lick of the sea, a love's length
From my shoes. The sand lay dark

Where the surf rushed and recoiled.
And at this border of briny and land,
I engraved certification in the softest cement.
With a wet finger as a pencil,
I brushed the bruise of her brand
And carved adoration in the sand.

ANGELA,
Six letters to loiter on this strand evermore.
Though I knew a high tide could censor my page,
I doubted, this moment, another moment could come.
But under stammering stars, a laundering liquid
Slithered a surf that nibbled my scribble

And asserted I'd only inserted AN.
I looked behind to the Del, to her gold,
Glowing skeleton and matronly pose.
I beseeched Del for a blessing.
She arose, dispatching her deed,
Inscribing her insignia.

Del reached out to the beach,
With one red fingering turret,
To sculpt in my sand,
To sketch on our strand.
We, she and I, etched
AND.

TORN RETINA

That February evening, I spied the full moon,
cracked as an egg. A tree limb splintered its light.
This image foretold my ghastly tomorrow,
when I see no C on the eyechart, not even big E.

Morning hatched another cracked egg
in my right eye, as though some stealthy spider
discarded her web in my socket,
dumped her silk in the pocket.

But blood tracked under the sheets of my cornea,
tracks quickly scattered by a brisk, brainy breeze.
Blood spurted to pose and then shatter
in cloudy debris.

This first shot of the war forecast the fusillade
to bloody the muddy pond in my vitreous.
Swirling soup vortexed in my vision.
On this day, I went blind on the right.

Doctor One said I've an eye that grew holey.
Just look at that rip in its pants.
Take your torn retina to deft Doctor Two.
And blindly, I traveled and somehow arrived,

where Doctor Two peeked
through the clouds in my eye
to register records
of my recently arrived retinal rectum.

I signed the consent
for the battle
and shook my fist at the cannons
of my bloodthirsty foe.

My champion fights cannon
with laser.
My army hurls argon and krypton
with punches

so hot they can sear my hung laundry,
retinal rags snapping in the wind,
until I am naked
no more.

One again, one again,
one again, punch,
till a hundred hot irons
branded my wound.

Each blast of the laser sprang
as singular as a snowflake

and as randomly wreathed
as the rims of a rainbow.

Amongst the clicks of flown bullets
and bouncing clacks of the reloads,
I winced when a shot splattered,
when the collision went deep.

A patch on my eye, and a prayer as I
left to be restful at home,
not knowing the outcome,
not knowing the allegiance of light

to ignite my unlighted lamp.
But I fancied the sun seeks
even one who is blind.
By and by, I pulled off the patch,

fearing the worst,
but our realm reentered my eye.
I see. I see all I can see.
I see He completely sees me.

I was once blind.
Now I behold the beyond,
the semblance suffusing sites that I enter,
garlanded by the grace of the Exemptor.

Now two worlds abide in two eyes.
The left espies as a child.
The right gapes, galactically wild.
If I unfurl the one, I unplug its partner.

Flares still go on blinking,
on the left side of my mind's manger,
and rubble falls
to the top of the chamber.

An eye lens launches upside-down light
to the retina. But we fancy we see it upright.
A lens inversion of image comes corrected,
though each glitch in the switch gets neglected.

I ask no more for transparency,
just a glance at God's glitter.
Now small blessings arouse me.
I glimpse grandiose gratuities granted.

SAUNA

Irradiate? No. *I radiate.*
All Finn words accent the first syllable.
I found flushed phonetics in the commodious fog
of my father's sauna.

I´ rrational.
I´ mmodest.
I´ mmoderate.
I´ ncandesce.

As cherished as church was our sauna.
Cloistered, I glimpsed my motion in mists
from my fortunate birth to a fleshy denouement.
My father and I vanished to visit in vapor,

in a blood-bubbling bath.
Purity, integrity, and nudity bloom
in the sauna, a love for the passage of time.
Time cannot hurry or wait in the sauna.

Practice the patience of stones on the stove.
We'd roused these rocks from the river,
chose the round and the rugged
from the riverbed to suffer the stove,

as a fiery frosting above the cake
that was baking
in a fire-foaming furnace,
aflame with wild wood.

The stones toted one thousand degrees.
They poured piety, flung forth in flames
to wash me in parched airs,
to cleanse me in hallowing flares.

We'd ripened these walls, one hour preheated,
broiling the benches, searing our saintly sweatshop
in volcanic vigor, till a roiling rapture rummaged
the pores of the poplar.

A bottle of broth may boil on my bench.
I endured, stronger than steam,
though water wends through us.
I dangled the dipper to harangue the hot rocks.

The prudent bring wooden ladles and pans,
but we always used metal, to question our hands.
Bare light from the dressing room window
framed a frosty abode to mock our searing asylum.

I hurled writhing rain upon rocks, rendering
the explosive protest, the restful unrest.

Though builders may make a city of saunas,
one thing I know: forever, the stove stays below.

For me, a half hour can drain every pore.
After more minutes of pause plodded past, I began
whisking my waggling capillaries, and, at last,
deep roasting was roosting in the church in my chest.

My dipper pitched splashing sprites down to caper,
effervescing my vexed veins in a vortex of vapor.
Many a saint has been soiled
and strayed from the canon of cleanness,

but in dry heat this night,
one disciple's wandering ways
got parboiled,
steamed to esteem.

A hot quiet, a dry fry,
can trigger tranquility,
can temper a tantrum
in sinews and soul.

Steam-cleaned amongst the baking birch leaves
was I, just a jug for the juices within me.
Only the ceiling got hotter,
in convection, not conviction.

When my steaming ghost finally fled
from the sauna, back to nippy November,
how that night quarreled with me!
And she pitched a prickling snowfall

at a broiling boy,
fresh from the hot box.
I sizzled the snowflakes alighting
on my naked before and behind.

I leapt and tortured a snowdrift.
Let November protest!
I fondled the frost to melt winter's dawn.
I evinced the yard light switched on.

Overhead, the moon had moved down,
another night to its journeys.
Moonglow rendered a reminder
of the Lord's stove and ladle beyond.

On that night and now another,
the moon and I still shine
upon a world licensed as yours
and a life lavished as mine.

SOUDAN MINE, MINNESOTA

My first day at Soudan, in 1906,
melting snow dazzled and danced
atop a rattling iron ore cart.
Water pimpled like gooseflesh
upon the ore cart's vibrations.

We'd wended watery ways,
a wife and two sons,
from the west coast of Finland
to Ellis, New York.
They trimmed my name

on the island
and shipped me
and my shopmates
to labor below and beyond
the lake called Vermilion.

Terra firma yet fosters
space underground,
where we hunted and hauled
out the red rocks that we found.
Never did I see the Iron Range

on a map,
but I've brushed a bucket
of red dust from my lap.
Ain't no elfin dwelling!
It's a real place that I'm telling.

Iron ores can pose as crystalline gems,
silvery gray in their luster.
But pound out their powder
and the true color comes through—
the rust-red of everything battered or bled.

My wife went to crying, the morning
that I went down the mine,
but I came out again,
down a furlong,
though it seemed like 'twas ten.

There were tears enough later
for miners.
I still favor the sunned side
of the sod, more than below,
near the reverse side of God.

I took enough of the language
to shovel and shout.
But to Eliina, it was Finnish

I broadcast.
When there's a school

for my boys,
they'll learn English,
so they won't work in the mine.
They'll work in the shine.
They'll work under a sign,

not work as the blind.
I'll toss a picture
of the iron ore mine at Soudan,
a thirty-story abode,
but with the top floor at the bottom.

Pray for no floods in the basement,
the top floor, I mean.
You don't know most of your neighbors,
except in the center elevator
that hoists your heart cords for cable.

Which floor is your exit
on the twenty-five levels?
Which of two diverged drifts
of rectangle or square?
You can always go right,

or then, you might even go left
if you fancy each path just as fair.
Everywhere, here, ends at out there.
You arrive at an inference
that it don't make no difference.

I dodged many a launch
of a loose rock falling down.
I walked as a caveman at war,
deep in the womb of the world.
In graywacke stones raining rubble,

I solicited trouble,
though my footfalls trudged trails
as steady as iron.
Just keep the lake and her rivers
from exploring my mine.

Iron ores look like carrots
on my first chance to see them,
but go to growing
a hundred feet wide.
Red rocks can sit up and stand down

like a carrot,
planted by hand, as if squeezed
in a gardener's garrote,

hidden in plain sight,
if you see through earth's hide,

hid like the wishes
in the spleen of a man,
wrapped in an envelope,
not for delivery.
One day, maybe, miners might burrow

to exhume our deepest desires.
Don't use your bare hands—
grab mine with your pliers.
I came after the gold rush
and was rushed to the rust rock.

Red irons parked patient,
but we're in a hurry to gather
the submerged volcanic volleys,
the frozen lava loaf lather,
and we packaged those ores

in one tock of a grandfather clock,
mined mystery of billion-year history.
But you find but one face on a clock.
Now try counting
the fathomless faces of rock.

Stone butchers, we,
swinging metal to meddle
with the spine of the ore,
and finding more bedrock in store
than mortal miners could go grinding.

I first worked under a soft hat
before helmets got hoisted
and worked by the hiss
of a hot carbide lamp,
fed the flame and protected

the refulgent reflector.
Knew my mates by the haste
of their nods.
They knew me by the pace
of my cervical cramp.

Those lamps on our helmets
bestowed halos on heads,
reminding me
that we were just visitors here,
not in our apprenticeship for dead.

You go down expecting the dark,
but discover more void than the veil
the blind burrow with braille.

No closet on Neptune
can lock out the light

and smother and douse
the mere thought of a spark,
as can Soudan mine, at noon,
in July, when church steeples
shine bright.

Frigid Soudan, Minnesota
reared risible rascals,
so Soudan got its name
from steaming Sudan,
an African hell,

where snow goes to fry.
Soudan sits as cold in her earth
as the soul of a hole,
but as true as the mine tower,
as bold as its bell.

It wasn't me as explorer,
prospector, tycoon,
who divined all the signs
for the Iron Range they first blessed,
then gathered us miners

as invited guests,
as a congregation upstairs
from Hades,
but downstairs from graveyards
of merchants and ladies.

It's my treasure, for as long as
the gravel glides in my spade.
Then the skip cart is owner,
and then the crusher takes over.
And we feed a furnace, after a ferry

in railcars and boats
to Cleveland and Gary.
Wish they'd send these mosquitoes
to steel mills in Pitt. Sixty yards down
and I swear in the dark I got bit.

I shed a skin in the years
we were called pioneers.
I lost a finger
and lost an infant, born cold.
But this mine saved my skin,

and its sod never sold
me to a boneyard
too close to the sun.

I lugged her nuggets, and maybe
I changed my mine's mind.

My twelve kids sprang up.
Half were hatched at Soudan.
In that Age, we couldn't see
a reason for resting nor stopping.
Now my grandsons got rich,

school-smart in the turf's topping.
But they ain't got no kids—
explain that one if you can.
Why's it the men in the pit
grow so genetically fit?

Seemed we blasted the drifts
into grittier gravel,
the farther aside
and the deeper we traveled.
But I felt cheer in digging below

because none ever dug to the top
of a celestial spire, not its crown.
Could be I'll walk
the world's circle and back
if we keep moving down,

if we keep on lighting
the black,
if we keep laying rails
for the buggies,
and fill the stope tunnels

with waste,
and divide each stope's sill
from its back,
and fit my own bad back
with a brace.

Worst was the work
in a raise, drilling,
then blasting, rock
right over your head.
The raise crew demolished

the rock from the roof,
then climbed up a ladder
to hand-loosen the shreds.
Four-foot nearer per blast
to the rock that is red.

I knew every step on that ladder
like I knew the beats of my breath.
A miner can't mine

if the rocks won't descend.
A miner just prays

rocks break like a chain
and go broken for certain,
and not in snaps like a curtain.
For all that, I felt grateful
to walk underground,

remembering the bygone miners,
the quarry, the horses, the hoists,
the pick shovels, pry bars,
and black powdered hands.
The old lifers, still digging,

and those departed by choice,
know something is stewing,
eternally brooding down there,
something coming and going
that's near dry and near moist.

After a blast, rock dust huddles
next to the candle.
You can't see your hand
on the cold prybar handle.
But upstairs, snow covers

the mined iron stockpile.
Stay dark under white.
Hide me from the light, so says
that red, subterranean child,
in terror denial.

In my dusty rock room,
too much for a dustbin,
too thick for a broom,
I'd name a favorite assignment,
the one that I sought.

With a huge, cabled scraper,
I dumped ore down the raise
and filled the lower apartment,
by its chimney side door,
until it became my new floor.

Drop it, don't lift.
Drop the ore
to earth's anchor.
Through the raise,
rocks leapt lower

and landed.
Waterpower lifted us
above rock to topsoil

in a hydraulic cage,
like I'm an actor on stage.

In a worked draft,
we sprayed water
to dust an explosion.
So, we kept the lunchroom
remote from the shaft.

The mine installed pipes
for water, electric,
signal, and air,
but every hour was eerie,
every minute a scare.

I didn't love every miner,
but I still see each as his face
and see him and his jacket
just where he stood in his place.
I can tell you no fat men

ever rode in those cages.
A few men ranked as bad,
certainly, badder than me. But all
were paid per pound of dug rock,
at rock-bottom wages.

Today, so I hear,
outside my old mine,
the old towers and cables
and rigs regally linger, long
after the crusher house carved

the last ore for the boats
at Two Harbors.
And say, if you visit,
take a tour of the township
and walk farther to stand

where I stood by the lake
called Vermilion.
Stand on the big boulder
as sunset approaches
and behold the bottomless ribbon

of red on the water,
as though in humble homage
to the blessed ore Sower
and the miners of iron,
the conquerors in Soudan.

A statue in Chisholm, a digger,
truly a dead ringer for me,
mines a memory of pitmen,

a reminder of concavity.
Just don't misremember

us miners of iron.
Men are mostly glassy
slag after smelting.
Don't remold us
as rugged as rock.

Blood and bones
ferry a tiny thimble
of iron, but carry
a cauldron of hurt,
a bucket of luck,

and a dab of drab dirt.
That jigger of iron
pours the precarious part,
the mettle in metal,
the red rocks in your heart.

THREE VISITS
WITH MY FATHER'S GRAVE

One.

Heaven cooled
and caressed my father's funeral.
A brittle, white November
snapped cracks across the sky.
My father seemed always larger
than the loft of all his labors.
This day, he narrowed to infinity,
to the forever, a neighborhood nearby.

My mother, my brother,
the family motored, chasing
the hearse, wherein, too,
my niece rode for the love of him,
riding with grandpa to the end,
to the end of all the rolling
upon the ragged road, on to a lavish lawn,
to encircling echoes that memories spawn.

Saintly snowflakes washed us.
Solemn snowfall sifted silence.
Calming coldness cradled gently
a somber journey to the grave.

I'd feel this damp dust forever.
I'm yet traveling in that throe,
waiting for the gates to show
and the heritor to wave.

Two.

August, I talked to my father's grave,
then to my father.
My tears might've pleased him,
in the old world.
Now, I fished for the feel of him,
when I brushed the green coat
of his carpet,
when I watched the wind

bend the grass.
Watched every stalk
stir in a sequence,
the way fur flutters,
the way cilia search,
the way water waves on the shore,
the way all the stadium lights
switch on together.

Clouds clustered
like manifest mountains,

as if now ascendable,
for a life so commendable.
My niece set up a wind chime
on his gritty, green grave.
The cryptic tones tinkled
a beauty that told me 'twas him.

I listened. I listened as a lad
and should've stood as a soldier.
But I grasped the chimes
and shook them for fun,
and brought naught
but a hollow earthly drum.
The wind paused.
The angels passed.

My father wondered
why I do these things.
I laid a rose upon his mantel
for memory, upon the portraiture
of paradise. For I cannot plant roses
upon his holy wind.
May the angels squire a choir
inspired by him, a holy hymn.

Three.

Town church bells tolled, a mile astray,
to grace my father's grave.
We stood beside the resting place,
beside the blessed base of stranded stories.
I brought along a friend, you see.
My father still accompanies me.
We sought to visit the entire family
and invade the realms of memory.

A dung beetle raced atop the grass,
fleeing me, perhaps, or marching
from the grips of graves and seeking
nicer neighbors, precincts known for scat.
Sparrows pranced atop a graveyard tree,
the only tree, a bedfellow quite misinformed
about the next-door noiseless fraternity,
about the constant curfew, the party sparsity.

My father, I mean he in me,
said, "Let's go."
"We can't leave yet," said I,
"I've not finished missing you."
I heard birds and beetles boasting,
near our sacrosanct conclave,
that Man is fated to fail famously
and destined for a grave.

"My tombstone blabs on one side,
only. The other side blinks blank.
Write upon that silent side.
Tell a tale or two."
I aimed to engrave an opus there,
to dispatch my dad's request.
I divulged a dozen dramas before
carving one I loved the best.

When we strolled back to the car,
my chaperone was love.
God gifts us each our fathers,
amidst our Father's reign above.
But Lord, pity the plight of Mankind,
creatures fashioned fit to seek Your signs.
You bequeathed Man a blessed blueprint, only,
and crayons to color betwixt Your lines.

HERE TO THERE

There, I flared, a tale in my lair,
a blueprint for high jinks, a sprite in the air.

Then Ma married Pa, and glob gobbled glob,
and I trekked from there over here at my job,

a here that is near, searingly, leeringly near,
always near. Near is never obscure.

Here, I and Ma shared a burgeoning affair
till I fled to somewhere, somewhere over there,

where there begat here, where I fostered a flair
for schoolwork, finally arriving at there.

From there, now here, I swear I circled a square.
I lost half my hair and drank beer, here and there.

Every new year reared fresh fear, over here,
though I steered clear of the sneerers who jeer

till I felt cheer in the here. At last, I'd never veer
from the man in the mirror.

Now abruptly they care. My syndrome is rare.
They offer a prayer. I sit in my wet underwear.

That gave them a scare. They don't even dare
share their only spare chair.

Doc says I'm rated to rank as belated,
finally crated, freighted, and migrated

to grounds that are gated, and Doc even stated
he's sad that I waited. My headstone is now dated.

I'm back home over there. No, you can't dodge
your next crib under the lawn of this lodge.

Ain't no use howling one foul diphthong or vowel.
Ain't no gratuity granting a third precinct to prowl.

Time parented just one punctilious pair.
You're either here or you're there.

You're either there in a hut or here in a hovel,
either learning to rot or learning to grovel.

But if I could tussle with Time,
like I can wring out a rhyme,

I'd tear off the "t" triggering here, I swear,
afore I'd tighten the "t" under here, over there.

KING'S KIN

Creation hides from chroniclers,
registrars of varnish on the void.
God launched His Holy Light—
not sun, His Lamp—upon day one.
This Light begat the gangplank
to load His galactic pioneers.
God paused the pilgrims' progress
till His decorating's done.

After Eden, Mankind made a mess
of anything attempted.
Blood, gore, and death deluged
Man's devil dealing deeds.
Though eyes espied stars' sparkles,
few fellows found the Light
that kindles darkness solely
when our harbor's Helmsman heeds.

God sought to script a sequel,
a story graced with glory, to remind
the blind that righteousness
resides within the Light. Christ
unveiled our God's great gangplank,
and sinners strolled the ship in Light,
though land's limp lamps, once bright,
writhed now, as nebulous as night.

Man has knocked upon each door
for wisdom, a comic quest, at best,
for Man excels at fudging facts,
Man's most enterprising sin.
Experts swing their flashlights.
Scholars strike a match. But Light
lit my soul in the hour the King
christened me His kin.

ABOUT THE AUTHOR

Hari Hyde is also the author of *The Honeygate Chronicles*, a satirical, fantasy adventure trilogy. Many readers who loved the lyrical style of those fables have forecast Hari Hyde's pilgrimage into poetry. Hari has harbored in Minnesota, the Milky Way, and the boisterous burrows of *Unbathed Brains*.

www.ingramcontent.com/pod-product-compliance
Lightning Source LLC
Chambersburg PA
CBHW020104310726

48970CB00002B/469